GIVEN UP . . .

We turned the corner, and I saw the asylum. If I didn't know better, it would have been the last place I'd have guessed was a Home, the last place for kids to live.

We reached the gate. A sign, black letters on white metal, was attached to it. The Hebrew Home for Boys. Ida pushed the gate open just as the clock struck ten. We trudged along a brick path to steps leading to a heavy wooden door.

Still holding me tight, Ida opened the door and a draft of cold air swooshed out, even colder than the air outside. We went in. The door thudded closed behind us and clicked shut. As soon as I heard the click I wanted to leave.

ALSO BY GAIL CARSON LEVINE

Ella Enchanted

The Princess Tales

The Fairy's Mistake
The Princess Test
Princess Sonora and the Long Sleep
Cinderellis and the Glass Hill

The Wish

DAVE AT NIGHT

GAIL CARSON LEVINE

HarperTrophy®
An Imprint of HarperCollinsPublishers

Harper Trophy® is a registered trademark of HarperCollins Publishers Inc.

Dave at Night
For information address HarperCollins Children's Books, a division of
HarperCollins Publishers, 1350 Avenue of the Americas, New York, NY 10019.

Library of Congress Cataloging-in-Publication Data
Levine, Gail Carson.
    Dave at night / Gail Carson Levine.
        p.   cm.
    Summary: When orphaned Dave is sent to the Hebrew Home for Boys
where he is treated cruelly, he sneaks out at night and is welcomed into the
music- and culture-filled world of the Harlem Renaissance.
    ISBN 0-06-028153-7 — ISBN 0-06-028154-5 (lib. bdg.)
    ISBN 0-06-440747-0 (pbk.)
    [1. Orphans—Fiction.   2. Jews—New York (N.Y.)—Fiction.   3. Harlem
Renaissance—Fiction.   4. Afro-Americans—Fiction.   5. New York (N.Y.)—
Fiction.]   I. Title.
PZ7.L578345Dav   1999   98-50069
[Fic]—dc21   .   CIP
                                                                          AC

Typography by Carla Weise
❖
First Harper Trophy edition, 2001
Visit us on the World Wide Web!
www.harperchildrens.com

To my father, the real Dave,
and to my mother.
You speak through me always.

ACKNOWLEDGMENTS

My deep thanks to Irving Aschheim for sharing the bounty of his encyclopedic memory; to Michael Stall and Hyman Bogen for helping me understand asylum life; to Jim Van Duyne for explaining the mysteries of classic luxury cars; to Steve Long of the Tenement House Museum for answering my questions about the Lower East Side and for directing my research into productive channels; to Kenny Kasowitz of the New York Transit Museum for telling me about travel by trolley and train in a younger New York City; to Nedda Sindin for her help with Yiddish and for her memories of New York City in the twenties; and to my friend and longtime colleague William Eller for his careful reading and insightful comments.

CHAPTER 1

From the start, I've always made trouble. My mama died of complications from having me. I once joked about it to my older brother, Gideon. I said I could make trouble even before I was born. Gideon thought I was serious because he said, "You didn't do it on purpose, Dave. You were too young. You weren't even yourself yet."

No, I didn't do it on purpose, but probably I was fooling around in her belly, having a fine time, and I kicked or punched too hard, and one thing led to another, and she died.

I had nothing to do with Papa dying, though. He died on Tuesday, October 26, 1926, when he fell off the roof of a house he was helping to build.

■ ■ ■

About four years before he died, when I was seven, I got in trouble for smearing glue on the chair of Izzy, the class bully. My stepmother, Ida, had to go to P.S. 42 and promise the principal that I'd never smear glue on anybody's chair ever again. I never did, but Ida had to visit P.S. 42 often anyway. I batted a ball into our fourth-grade teacher's rear end (by accident—my aim wasn't *that* good). I fought with Izzy on the stairs. I let a mouse loose in our classroom. And more. Some things I didn't do but got blamed for because I'd done everything else.

Papa tried to be mad when I got into trouble. "You have to behave," he'd say.

I'd say, "Yes, Papa."

"Ida can't do her work if she has to go to school because of you."

"I know." Ida made ladies' blouses on the sewing machine next to her and Papa's bed.

"This is the end of it, then. Yes?"

"Yes, Papa."

"Good." Then he always asked, "What happened?"

At the beginning of my story, he'd listen and frown, but then the frown would disappear and his shoulders would start to shake. A little while later he'd be laughing and wiping tears from his eyes.

Papa was a woodworker. Before he came to the United States, he made a cabinet for the sultan of Turkey. The sultan was so pleased with the three hidden drawers Papa put into it that he gave Papa a gold medal.

Whenever he told about the medal, Papa would laugh. "We had to come to this country because of the sultan," he'd say. "I didn't want any more work from him. If he liked what you did, he gave you a medal. If he didn't like it . . ." Papa would drag a finger across his throat. ". . . Too bad for you." He'd laugh some more and add, "When we came to New York City, I sold the medal and bought your mama a dress."

But this wasn't the real reason Papa came to the United States. The real reason was too serious for him to talk about, so he'd joke about his medal instead. The truth was that there had been a war, and Greece had taken over the city where he lived. Papa and his family, the Caros family, had sided with Turkey, and so they all moved here when Greece won.

The day Papa died, I was late getting home after school. Detention and then stickball. When I got there, Gideon was sitting on the steps outside our building. As soon as I saw him, I knew something was wrong. He was never out here. He was always upstairs or at the library, studying. When I got close enough, I saw he had been crying.

"What happened?"

"Papa . . ."

I ran into the building. Gideon followed me.

Papa was in the front room, lying on the couch where Gideon and I slept at night. He wasn't bleeding, but he didn't look right. He looked like Papa in a photograph, not like Papa. His face was too white, with gray shadows under his eyes and on his cheeks.

"Papa!"

He didn't move. Ida stood at the window, looking out. She didn't turn when I came in. Mrs. Stern from across the hall stood next to her, patting her back.

"I hit a home run, Papa. We won the game." I nudged his shoulder. His arm swung off the edge of the couch. His fingers dangled a few inches above the floor.

I knew he was dead then, but I said to Gideon, "Did Papa break his arm?" And then I said to Papa, "I'll make you laugh so it won't hurt." But I couldn't think of anything funny. Then I remembered an old joke. "What did the caterpillar say to the boa constrictor?"

"Dave . . ." Gideon said.

Mrs. Stern left Ida and started toward me. She was going to hug me and I didn't want her to.

"No. Listen. Papa wants to hear it. The caterpillar said, 'I don't want to be around when *you* turn into a butterfly.'" I laughed. "Do you get it, Papa?" I leaned down and said right into his ear, "Isn't it funny? Don't you get it?"

From where she stood, Ida said, "Don't *you* get it? He's dead."

Mrs. Stern turned me away from Papa and held me. I stood stiffly against her.

Ida went on talking. "In six months we would have moved out of here. We almost had enough saved up."

I pulled away from Mrs. Stern and ran out of the house.

Gideon caught up with me after I'd gone a block. "Where are you going, Dave?"

I didn't answer him. I was heading for Seward Park to see if anyone was still playing stickball. When I got there, my friends were gone, but our stick was still lying on the ground. I found a ball under the Nash that was parked on Essex Street.

"I'll show you how I got the homer." I threw the ball in the air and swung at it. I missed. I swung again and missed. And again. And again. Once Gideon told me to stop, but I wouldn't. I kept swinging and missing. I started to cry.

"Why can't I hit it?" I said. "What's wrong with me?"

"You'll get it if you keep trying." Gideon was crying too.

"Why are *you* crying? You're not even trying to hit it." I laughed in the middle of crying. Then I connected. Crack.

Papa was dead.

The ball didn't go far. The stick, when I threw it with all my might, went farther and crashed into the brick wall outside the boys' toilet.

I crouched down and cried, really cried. I pictured Papa at breakfast, dipping bread into his coffee, the bread making his cheek bulge while he chewed. I pictured him before he left the house, trying to kiss Ida good-bye and her pushing him away. I pictured him tossing his hat in the air and positioning himself under it, so it landed square on his head. I pictured him saying good-bye to me and Gideon the way he always did. "Good-bye, genius" to Gideon. "Good-bye, rascal" to me.

And then he went out, back straight, looking taller than he really was. Looking happy, because Papa was always happy. And now he was dead. He wouldn't be happy about being dead.

I stopped thinking. I just kept yelling in my brain, "Papa," over and over. And crying.

CHAPTER 2

$\mathcal{A}$FTER A LONG time I noticed that my calves were aching and I was cold. I stood up. Gideon was looking at the sky.

"It should be raining," he said.

"Yeah." I knew what he meant.

"Let's go home," Gideon said. "Ida will worry."

She wouldn't, and Gideon knew it. Mrs. Stern from across the hall would be more likely to worry about us than Ida. President Coolidge would be more likely to worry about us than Ida.

When we got home, the apartment was empty. Ida wasn't there, and Papa was gone too.

"Gideon!" I said. "Maybe he wasn't dead. Maybe he woke up."

I pictured it. Papa sits up. He groans, "What happened? I feel like a sack of potatoes." He looks around for us. "Where are Dave and Gideon?" Ida says, "How should I know? We thought you were dead." And Papa says, "Dead? I'm not dead." He laughs. "I'd feel better if I was dead."

Gideon said, "He's dead. He broke his neck."

Ida came in. "They took him to the funeral home. We'll bury him tomorrow." She went to the icebox and took out a bowl covered with a dishrag. "And then what? After the funeral, then what?"

Then what? Papa would stay dead and be dead forever.

I didn't pay attention to the rabbi during the funeral. I counted thirty-four people—our neighbors, my aunts and uncles, and some people I didn't know who were probably older cousins. The cousins who were around my age weren't there. I guess they were in school.

The rabbi's eyebrows were so bushy they stuck out an inch in front of his face. I was sitting next to Ida. Her bony hands were folded in her lap. She stared at the rabbi and never moved.

Papa must hate being up there in the coffin, I thought, not even able to wink at the relatives who came to stare at him.

The cemetery was in Queens. We followed the hearse in a Packard limousine. It was the first time I'd ever been in an automobile. I'd never been to Queens before either. It was the first time for a lot of things—my first time in a cemetery, and the first time for burying my father.

I wished I could see how fast we were going, but the driver was hunched over the speedometer.

"Do you think we're doing forty?" I whispered to Gideon as streets and houses whooshed past us.

He just stared out the window. Ida sat looking into her lap. Unless she did it while I was asleep, she hadn't cried for Papa.

I looked around the inside of the car. The floor was covered with a dark green carpet, and the walls were covered with dark green cloth. I reached across to the back of the chauffeur's seat and folded out the jump seat. Ida ignored me. Gideon watched, then turned back to the window. I crossed over and sat down. I figured I might never have another chance. I liked the way Second Avenue looked, flying backwards away from me. I wondered if hearses came this way often. Up Coffin Avenue. Right turn on Corpse Street. Continue down Goner Row. Left turn to Dead Man Boulevard.

At Twenty-third Street we went under the el, and we stayed under it all the way across the Queensboro Bridge. A train thundered above us as we crossed. It shook the bridge and rattled my teeth.

Queens didn't look like part of New York City. It had lots of empty fields and wooden houses. Hey, look at that—a yard full of tombstones. The Riley Bros. tombstone factory. Dead people were big business in Queens. I turned around to look out the front window. Ahead of us, the hearse rolled on, feeling right at home.

A few minutes later we turned and drove into the

cemetery. The car stopped next to a freshly dug hole, and we got out. I stamped my feet to stay warm while the rabbi said a prayer.

After they lowered the coffin into the hole, we all had to throw dirt on it. I wouldn't have been able to do it, except I pretended Papa wasn't in there. The coffin held a pair of huge, long shoes. It didn't matter, throwing dirt on shoes.

When we got home, we heard voices as we climbed the stairs. Ida opened our door, and I saw that almost everybody who'd come to the funeral was crowded into our front room. The noise was so loud—talking, laughing—that no one noticed us till Ida started pushing through the crowd.

Aunt Sarah, who was standing near the doorway, hugged Gideon and then me. She kept an arm around my shoulders while she said, "I can't believe Abe's dead. He should be here."

Uncle Jack, who was visiting from Chicago where he lived, said, "He had such a brain. He could add a column of figures in his head and come out right every time." Uncle Jack put his hand on Gideon's head. "This genius can probably add two columns." Uncle Jack was Gideon's favorite relative. Gideon had been heartbroken when he had moved away last year.

I left Aunt Sarah and wandered between the clumps of people, listening. I heard about a banana-eating contest Papa had once won. I heard what an artist he was, how perfect everything he made was. They told the story about the sultan and the medal again.

Aunt Lily was telling about the time Papa had brought a goat to school. She was my mama's sister. She and Aunt Sarah, Papa's sister, boarded with a family a few blocks from us.

I heard a bang. Everybody stopped talking. Across the room, Ida was pounding her fist against the wall. Plaster trickled down from the ceiling onto the sofa.

"Abe's dead," she yelled. "Who cares what happened twenty-five years ago?" She banged the wall again. "I can't keep these boys." Bang. "I can't feed them." She stopped pounding. "Who wants them?"

She was giving us away. As if she owned us. I don't want my hat anymore. Who's interested? I don't want Gideon and Dave anymore. Who's interested?

Where was Gideon? I looked for Uncle Jack. There he was, pressing a chunk of ice to his temple for the headache he always had. Gideon stood next to him. We stared at each other.

"Don't talk that way," Aunt Sarah said. "You and Abe had savings. You'll manage."

Uncle Milt said, "Gideon and Dave will help, and you'll find more boarders soon."

Till last month, three brothers—Sy, Al, and Max Rubino—had slept on mats in the front room with Gideon and me. But then they had moved to their own apartment in the Bronx.

"How many boarders can I take?" Ida shouted. "The savings won't last. You try feeding two boys on what I earn. Who wants them?"

Nobody said anything. Then Aunt Sarah said there wasn't any room where she and Aunt Lily lived.

Cousin Melvin said he was out of work and out of money.

Uncle Milt said Aunt Fanny was too sick.

Great-Aunt Rae was too old.

Uncle Irving had seven children already.

Then Uncle Jack said, "Gideon can come home with me."

Gideon! What about me?

"Who'll take Dave?" Ida said.

Gideon whispered something to Uncle Jack. He shook his head.

It was quiet again. Then Aunt Lily began to whisper to Aunt Sarah. I knew it was about me, but I didn't want to live with them and the whole Cohen family. I wanted to go with Gideon.

Aunt Lily stopped whispering and didn't say they'd take me. Nobody wanted me. Well, I didn't want them either. Or Ida. I walked across the room toward the kitchen. I didn't want to stay in here with everybody.

As I left, I heard Aunt Sarah say, "If you give him up, Ida, he'll have a hard time."

What did she mean, give me up? If nobody wanted me, who would she give me to?

CHAPTER
3

I SAT AT the kitchen table. Someone had covered
it with the crocheted tablecloth my mama had
made, which we only used on the High Holy Days.
It was all we had of Mama's. When she died, Papa had
given her clothing to Aunt Lily.

Gideon would talk Uncle Jack into taking me.
Gideon was smart enough to convince you that turtles
could fly, so he'd be able to convince his favorite uncle
not to leave me behind. And if he couldn't, then he'd
say he wasn't going. He'd say he was sticking with his
brother.

There was food on the table, brought by the relatives. I ate a Sephardic egg, which was a hard-boiled
egg cooked for hours with coffee grounds and onion
skins. Usually they were delicious, but this one had no
taste.

The relatives were talking softly in the front room—softly till Ida hollered, "You want me to starve? And him too?"

There was silence, then some murmuring, and then Uncle Milton came into the kitchen to say good-bye. He hugged me and put a dime in my hand. "Who knows?" he said. "It may come in handy." He left, and Great-Aunt Rae hobbled in. She gave me a nickel. Except for Uncle Jack, they all came to me, one or two at a time, and they all slipped money into my pocket or into my hand—mostly quarters and dimes, a few nickels, and no pennies.

Uncle Jack stayed after everyone left. I went back into the front room. Gideon was packing. I couldn't believe it. He was going without me. Ida was sitting on the bed in her and Papa's bedroom, her skinny shoulders hunched over. I could see her from where I sat on the couch.

Gideon and Uncle Jack were going to sleep at Cousin Melvin's tonight and leave for Chicago tomorrow. Uncle Jack stood at the window, holding more ice to his temple. It was late afternoon, starting to get dark out.

Uncle Jack didn't say anything. He and Gideon were the only quiet ones in the Caros family. Normally Ida hardly ever talked, either, but she wasn't really a Caros.

It wouldn't take Gideon long to pack. Neither of us had much. I sat on the couch, tossing my green rubber ball from one hand to the other. Gideon kept looking at me and not saying anything.

"I can be just as quiet as Gideon," I told Uncle Jack. "I wouldn't make any noise if I lived with you. I wouldn't give you headaches."

"Dave is determined," Gideon said. "If he puts his mind to it, he can do anything."

Uncle Jack shook his head. "Dave is too much of a handful for me."

I wouldn't be. I'd be good.

"If the factory weren't so noisy, I'd take him." Uncle Jack was the bookkeeper in a place that made printing presses. "When I get home, I need peace and quiet." He moved the ice to the other temple. "Abie always boasted about the two of you—brilliant Gideon and daredevil Dave."

"Dave's a good boy," Gideon said.

"I know he is." Uncle Jack turned to Ida, who had gotten up and was standing in the doorway. "In a year or so when he's older, I'll send for him if I can."

What a laugh, him making excuses to Ida. What was *her* excuse? But that was that. He wouldn't take me. I bounced my green ball as hard as I could. Let his head hurt.

I bet Gideon was secretly glad to be going without me, the troublemaker. I bet he couldn't wait to get to Chicago and start being quiet with Uncle Jack.

Gideon closed the suitcase and went back to the bureau. He took out his treasure, the best thing he had, the carving of animals marching onto Noah's ark that Papa had made for him. "Here, Dave. You keep it."

I took it. I didn't say thanks or give him anything to remember me by. Let him leave. I didn't care if I never saw him again.

"You'll be all right," Gideon said. "You always are."

Sure I'd be all right. What did that have to do with anything?

"Ready?" Uncle Jack asked.

"Ready."

Uncle Jack bent over and hugged me. "I'll send for you when you're older."

I didn't hug him back.

"Good-bye, Dave," Gideon said. "I'll write."

"Where will you send the letter?" I muttered.

"What?" he said.

I shook my head. Good riddance.

"Good-bye," he said again. "Don't make trouble."

They left, closing the door softly behind them.

I sat on the couch. I thought about asking what Aunt Sarah had meant about giving me up, but I didn't do it. I wouldn't give Ida the satisfaction.

I did ask if I could go play stickball. She said I couldn't. She said we were sitting shiva. Sitting shiva means you stay home for a week after somebody dies. You sit around in torn clothing to show how sad you are, and people visit you to pay their respects.

Nobody else came that day. For dinner we ate the baked fish and the spinach pie that Aunt Lily and Aunt Sarah had brought. After dinner I drew funny pictures of the kids at school for a while. Then I started bouncing

my green ball. After two bounces, Ida told me to stop.
So I practiced snapping the fingers of my left hand. I
was starting to get it when Ida told me I was driving her
crazy. So I just sat, holding Gideon's carving on my lap,
tracing the shapes Papa had dug into it.

The carving was on a board of cherry wood about
a foot and a half wide and about nine inches high. Papa
hardly ever got a piece of fine wood like that, so he'd
saved it for something special. Then, ten years ago
when Gideon was four years old, he became so sick that
everybody thought he'd die. Papa stayed with him, and
while he waited for Gideon to get better or to die, he
made the carving.

Forty-eight animals marched up the plank or waited
in line to get on the boat. You couldn't see the whole
ark, just one end of it and the bottom of the sails. You
couldn't see every animal entirely either, because some
were partly blocked by others. For example, all you
could see of the elephants were two trunks, part of a
tusk, and one big floppy ear. But you saw a whole leopard, padding fearsomely up the plank. Riding on the
leopard's back, knowing he was safe for the moment,
was a monkey eating a banana. And playing around
the leopard's feet were two fat mice. Behind the animals
and the boat was a giant wave with the foaming crest
all the way at the top of the board.

Following the animals, at the very end of the line,
were the humans—a man holding a small boy by the
hand and a woman carrying a baby. The man was Papa.

I could tell by his curly beard and the striped scarf around his neck. The boy was Gideon and the baby was me. The woman wasn't Ida, because she and Papa didn't even meet till I was three. Besides, Ida was tall and skinny with frizzy hair. The woman in the carving was shorter than Papa, and she was plump, and she was smiling. The woman was my mother before she died from having me.

When I went to bed I put the carving in my bureau drawer, next to the wooden cigar box that was my treasure box. Inside it were my green rubber ball, my five marbles, the money the relatives had given me, and a scrap of wood I'd tried to whittle into the shape of a leopard like the one in the carving.

I slept for a few hours and then woke up and couldn't fall back asleep. I was used to having Gideon next to me, and I missed—not him, I didn't miss him—I missed his breathing. I hoped he wasn't sleeping either. I hoped he was lying on the floor. I hoped he had a rock for a pillow. I hoped a rat would bite him. He could write a hundred letters. I wouldn't read any of them.

In the bedroom, Ida snored softly. I wondered if Gideon understood what Aunt Sarah had meant about giving me up. I wondered if that was why he wouldn't stay. Maybe it meant sending me to Salonika, where Papa and Mama had come from. Mama's brother still lived there. Ida might write to him and see if he'd take me. She wouldn't get an answer any time soon. By then she'd know that it didn't cost much to feed me, and maybe she'd let me stay here. Not that I wanted to live with her, but I did want to go on playing stickball in the park and drawing pictures and fighting with Izzy and making trouble in school.

The apartment was too empty without Papa and Gideon. I got up and went into the hall to the toilet. I knocked on the door and waited a few seconds before I went in. You never knew, even in the middle of the night. Mr. Engle, who boarded with the Sterns across the hall, had a bad stomach.

When I came out of the toilet, I went downstairs. I was only in my underpants and my undershirt. I stepped out into the street. The sidewalk was cold under my bare feet and the air was chilly. But I didn't want to go back upstairs.

Papa wouldn't want me out here. He'd worry that I'd catch cold. But he'd think it was funny that I wasn't dressed. I spread my arms. I was a ghost. Like Papa. No, Papa wasn't a ghost. He was just dead.

I heard the *clop clop* of a horse and cart on Canal Street. Our street was empty. I couldn't believe anybody lived in the buildings, they were so quiet.

Only the candy store on the corner was open. The light from its window spilled into the street. I walked around it, staying in the shadow. Mr. Goldfarb was alone inside, leaning on the counter and reading a newspaper. I turned the corner onto Grand Street. The appetizing store was closed. The barrels of pickles that sat on the sidewalk during the day were inside for the night. I tried the door, but it was locked. Too bad. I could have gone in and had a feast—some smoked fish, a few pickles, and, for dessert, dried fruit and pistachios. I could have paid Mr. Schwartz later out of the money the relatives gave me.

I found three pear wrappers, not at all muddy, in the street outside the appetizing store. I picked them up and held them carefully. People fight over them because fruit wrappers are softer than anything else for wiping your backside.

I was freezing, so I turned back. Upstairs, Ida was still sleeping. I rolled myself up in the blanket. If Gideon went to Chicago without me, or to Australia, I didn't care. I could have more fun without him. He would never go outside in his underwear.

When nobody was sitting shiva with us, Ida sewed blouses. I hated staying in the house, but she wouldn't let me go out and play. Most of the time I drew in my school notebook. I copied the animals from Papa's carving, or I drew faces. Once, I accidentally drew Gideon's face. I turned him into a girl with long hair and smoochy lips.

Sometimes I couldn't sit still. Then I tried to teach myself to walk on my hands, till Ida told me to stop. I did somersaults across the front room, till Ida told me to stop. I hopped on one foot, till Ida told me to stop.

On Monday my friend Ben Weiss came with his mother.

"What's going on at school?" I asked him.

"Nothing."

"Did we win any stickball games?"

He shook his head. "Sammy's been playing first."

Sammy! He ducked if a ball looked at him cross-eyed.

Ben fished in his pocket and pulled out a marble. "I found it in the gutter outside of school. You can have it."

It was a beauty, a cloudy yellow-white with a swirl of purple. "Thanks." Papa dies and people keep giving me things—money, marbles, the carving.

"Izzy beat Sammy up."

"We have to go." Mrs. Weiss stood up. "I have to start cooking."

"He gave him a shiner and a nosebleed," Ben whispered. Then he said out loud, "See you in school."

Maybe. Maybe not.

Aunt Lily and Aunt Sarah came on Tuesday. I didn't ask Aunt Sarah what she had meant about giving me up. I didn't want to in front of Ida. Aunt Sarah didn't say anything about it either. Probably she thought Ida had forgotten and she didn't want to bring it up. But I knew Ida hadn't forgotten. She didn't forget anything that had to do with money. She remembered the exact number of blouses she couldn't make each time she had to go to school because of me. She remembered every penny Papa ever lost at pinochle. So she wouldn't forget giving me up. If she could have sold me, I'd have been gone before Papa was dead an hour.

CHAPTER 4

WHEN I WOKE up on Wednesday morning, Ida was packing my clothes into a suitcase. Papa was dead a week, shiva was over, and she was giving me up.

I pretended I was still asleep and watched her. There wasn't much to pack, only the suit I wore to Papa's funeral, a change of underwear, Gideon's cast-off knickers that didn't fit me yet, and my winter coat, which was too short in the arms and which barely buttoned across my chest. She didn't pack Papa's carving or my treasure box, so I got up and put them on top of my clothes. I didn't ask where I was going. Wherever it was, it would be an improvement.

The suitcase was Papa's banged-up big one, which he'd brought with him to this country. If I'd owned anything heavy, it would have gone right through the worn fiberboard covering.

Ida snapped the suitcase shut. "I'm sorry, Dave," she said, straightening up, "but I can't buy food and pay the rent by myself. If I don't have you, I can be a boarder somewhere."

I nodded.

"Abe would understand."

He would never understand. But I did. She was a louse. And Gideon was a louse. And Uncle Jack and my other relatives were lice.

"You'll have enough to eat at the Home."

Home? *The* Home? She meant—

"Let's go. The orphanage is . . ."

I was a fool never to have thought of it before. I never even thought of myself as an orphan, but what else was I?

An orphanage. Papa would die all over again if he knew.

But maybe it would be better to be an orphan in an orphanage than an orphan living with Ida.

Maybe not.

The orphanage was way uptown. We had to take the subway, thirteen blocks away on Lafayette Street. As we walked, I said good-bye to the neighborhood. In my mind, not out loud, I said good-bye to Ike, the produce peddler who was hollering about his juicy lemons. Good-bye to the Turkish candy peddler and his delicious halvah. Good-bye to the horse, stamping its feet in front of the dry-goods cart. Good-bye to the laundry hanging out a million windows. To the roasted-corn man, and the sweet smell of his corn. To the cobblestones I was walking on. To the street cleaner's wooden wagon. To the train roaring above us on Allen Street. To the peddler who tugged at Ida's sleeve, trying to get her to buy a scrub brush. Good-bye to the pickle store, to the sour pickles my friend Ben had taught me to love. Good-bye to Ben too.

We came to the Bowery, the end of our neighborhood. On the other side of the avenue, things were the same but different, and I stopped saying good-bye. The streets were just as crowded and noisy, but lots of the signs were in Italian, and most of the shouting was too. We passed a peddler selling clams and one selling roasted chickpeas, which you never saw near us.

It took us three trains to get uptown. During the ride I had only one thought: I wouldn't stay at the Home if I didn't like it.

We got off the subway at 137th Street, and Ida clamped her hand on my arm. We climbed up the subway stairs and the Home was the first thing I saw, the biggest thing around, made of red bricks that went on forever.

Broadway was quieter than the streets in my old neighborhood. There were stores, but only one peddler's wagon, and a tenth as many people.

There was no entrance to the orphanage on Broadway.

We walked next to it along 136th Street. The building, surrounded by a high iron fence, stretched all the way to the next avenue, which was Amsterdam. The handle of my suitcase was loose, and the suitcase banged into my knee whenever I took a step. Ida offered to carry it, but I didn't want any favors from her.

It was chilly, and I wished I'd worn my coat. We turned the corner, and I saw the front of the asylum. My eyes traveled up to where a pointy tower rose, like a witch's hat, three stories above the entrance. Below the tower was a clock, and on each side of the clock was a smaller pointy tower. The whole building was only four stories high in the highest part, the middle section. The rest was just three, but each story was very tall. The building wasn't made for people. It was made for witches, with plenty of room for their hats.

If I didn't know better, it would have been the last place I'd have guessed was a Home, the last place for kids to live.

We reached the gate. A sign, black letters on white metal, was attached to it. The Hebrew Home for Boys. Ida pushed the gate open just as the clock struck ten. We trudged along a brick path to steps leading to a heavy wooden door.

Still holding me tight, Ida opened the door and a draft of cold air swooshed out, even colder than the air outside. We went in. The door thudded closed behind us and clicked shut. As soon as I heard the click I wanted to leave.

The lobby was bigger than in a movie theater. Next to the door were two long windows. Across from them a marble staircase led up to a balcony. To my left and right were long corridors lined with doors. The floor was black-and-white tiles, and the walls were stone up to my shoulders. Above that they were painted gray-green, all the way up to a faraway gray-green ceiling.

Somewhere someone sneezed, and the sneeze echoed off the stone walls. I shivered.

The lobby was empty. No orphans except me.

"Where do I go?" Ida said.

"You can leave," I said. "I don't need you." I'd wait a minute or two and then leave too.

She ignored me. I heard footsteps and the echo of footsteps. A man entered the far end of the right-hand corridor. Ida walked me toward him.

"Pardon me," she called. She whispered, "If you get in trouble here, I can't take you back."

Fine with me. Excellent with me.

The man walked toward us. He was tall and thin, but when he got close enough I saw that his face was pudgy. His smile looked out of place, like it wasn't used to being on his face.

"I telephoned," Ida said. "His father died, and I can't keep him, but he's a—"

"That's all right. We'll take good care of him." He turned the smile on me. "How old are you?"

"Eleven," Ida said before I could figure out what I wanted to tell him. "He's a good—"

"Ah. I have the elevens. I'm your prefect, young man. You'll see a lot of me. I'll tuck you in at night."

And I'll yank your nose off.

He said his name was Mr. Meltzer. He said he'd take us to an office where Ida could sign the papers to give me away. But he didn't take us anywhere. He just stood there, smiling.

"I don't have any money to give you," Ida said.

The smile disappeared. "Follow me," he barked.

The office was a short way into the left-hand corridor. Inside, three men sat at wooden desks. It was as cold in here as it was in the hall. Each man wore a woolen vest under his suit jacket. The room stank from cigar smoke.

Mr. Meltzer explained to the man at the first desk that Ida was here to give me up. The man opened his desk and pulled out three sets of papers.

"You'll have to sign these," he said.

Ida let go of my arm, but Mr. Meltzer was between me and the door. She leaned down to sign and then straightened up. "Good-bye, Dave. If I were Rockefeller, I'd keep you and Gideon."

If I were Babe Ruth, I'd play for the Yankees.

At least she didn't try to kiss me. She turned to the man at the desk and started signing.

"Come with me," Mr. Meltzer barked at me.

This was my chance. Ida thought she could give me away. Well, she couldn't. I picked up the suitcase and held it in my arms, although I could barely reach around it. If it was in my arms he couldn't hold my hand. "The handle's loose," I said.

He held the door open for me, then started down the corridor, away from the lobby. I tried to walk silently, so he wouldn't notice if I wasn't next to him anymore. But my shoes clicked on the tile floor. As I walked, I stepped out of them. My socks were silent, beautifully silent. I took a few more steps forward. Then I turned and ran.

CHAPTER 5

"HEY, YOU!"

I had almost reached the lobby. I heard Mr. Meltzer pounding after me. The suitcase was slowing me down. I dropped it and sprinted for the door.

The carving! My treasure box! I wheeled and dashed back. But before I got to the suitcase, Mr. Meltzer grabbed me. I struggled to reach it. If I could get it, I'd swing it into him. I'd knock him over and run.

"Stay still, you brat," he panted.

I fought harder, but he held on. I couldn't get away.

"Now come." He walked me to my shoes and waited while I put them on. Then he walked me to the suitcase. "Pick it up." He held my shoulders and eased me down to it without letting go for a second.

He marched me back up the corridor to a door at

the end. It opened onto an ordinary wooden staircase, not marble like the one in the lobby. We climbed up to the top floor, the third. It was slightly warmer up here, but the echoing silence was the same, and so was the ugly gray-green paint job on the walls.

Mr. Meltzer stopped in front of a door and opened it while holding on to me. Inside was a nurse's office with a scale and a cot and the nurse's desk, which had a telephone on it. The nurse said hello and smiled like there was something to smile about. She weighed me, listened to my heart, and looked in my ears. When she riffled through my hair for lice, she said, "I wish I had curls like yours." She asked me if I'd had the mumps, measles, chicken pox. I told her no, but I'd had hoof-and-mouth disease when I was eight. She laughed, which surprised me. Mr. Meltzer didn't, which didn't.

She asked me if I had any brothers or sisters. I told her my brother had died in the same accident that killed Papa.

When she finished examining me, she told me not to put my clothes back on. "How old are you? Nine?"

I said I was fourteen. Mr. Meltzer said I was eleven.

"Small for your age." She went to a closet and came back carrying a pile of clothes and a pair of low boots. "A new wardrobe."

"I like the clothes I came in with."

"Put on the uniform." Mr. Meltzer folded my old things and put them in my suitcase.

"We all wear uniforms here," the nurse said.

Yeah, but her uniform showed she was a nurse. Mine would show I was an orphan.

The yellowy-white shirt was too big. I wondered if the kid who'd had it before me was still alive.

The tie had gray-green and purple stripes. The gray knickers were too big. I had to buckle the belt on the last hole to keep them up. The gray jacket was too big and it had no pockets. The knickers and the jacket were stiff enough for a coat of armor. Scratchy too. The heels of the white socks came up to my ankles. Only the shoes fit.

"Orphans may come and orphans may go," the nurse said, "but their clothing lasts forever."

Mr. Meltzer picked up my suitcase and we left the nurse's office. In the hall, he said he was going to take me to meet Superintendent Bloom, who was in charge of the whole orphanage. "Call him *sir*. He's not as nice as I am."

Back downstairs, Mr. Meltzer knocked on the first door to the right of the lobby.

"Come in," a rumbly voice called.

It was warm in his office. Not hot. Just right.

Mr. Bloom was huge. His chest and head loomed over his desk like the Hebrew Home for Boys loomed over Broadway. He pushed back his chair and stood up. Scraping against the wall on the way, he walked around to my side of his desk and bent down to inspect me through thick spectacles. He smiled, showing a million teeth.

He looked up at Mr. Meltzer, who was leaning against the door so I couldn't get out. "What's his name?"

He could have asked me. Didn't he think I knew my own name?

"Dave Caros," Mr. Meltzer said.

"Dave, you have my sympathy for your loss."

What did I lose? Oh. Papa.

"But no loss comes without gain. I like my boys to think of me as their papa." Mr. Bloom's smile disappeared. "A stern papa, because all good fathers are stern."

I'd never think of this gorilla as my papa.

"Look around this office," Mr. Bloom went on. "Take a good look."

I looked. The room was oak-paneled. A telephone hung on the wall to the left of the desk. An electric log glowed in the fireplace on the opposite wall. A knick-knack case stood next to the fireplace. It was very fine, like something Papa could have made. The door had small glass panes separated by wooden latticing.

"That's enough," Mr. Bloom said. "You don't want to be in this office again. Only bad boys see this office twice, and you're not a bad boy, are you?"

I was supposed to say something. "I'm a good boy."

"You're not a bad boy?" he repeated, frowning. His glasses slipped sideways on his greasy nose.

I already told him I wasn't.

He reached behind him for the yardstick on his

desk. What had I done? I turned to Mr. Meltzer, but he was looking at his shoes.

He must be deaf. I spoke louder. "I'm a good boy."

He raised the yardstick.

Then I remembered. "Sir, I'm a good boy, sir." Some papa.

"Glad to hear it." He put the yardstick down. "Welcome to the Home."

We left the office and I felt cold again. Mr. Meltzer took me to the end of the hall and around the corner. He opened the third door on our right. A roomful of boys dressed like me turned their heads to stare. The teacher said, "Another one!"

Mr. Meltzer pulled me to a desk toward the back. I sat, keeping my eyes on my suitcase.

"New boy. Name's Dave Caros." Mr. Meltzer turned to leave.

"My suitcase . . ." I said, starting to stand.

"It'll be under your bed." He left.

It better be.

The boy on my left was bouncing up and down in his seat. His right hand jerked from the inkwell to his notebook and back again. His left hand drummed on the side of the desk, while both his knees pumped up and down. I leaned over and looked in the notebook. He was drawing violins. The page was full of ink blotches and smudges and, in between, violins.

"New boy," the teacher called. He was short and almost bald—just a few gray hairs held in place with pomade. "I'm Mr. Gluck. Supplies are in your desk." He went to a map of North America that was tacked to the wall next to the blackboard. "Stand up and show us what a scholar you are."

I stood. The boy on my other side started coughing.

"What state is this?" Mr. Gluck tapped the map with his pointer.

"New Jersey."

That cough sounded bad. If I had a cough like that, Papa would have made me inhale steam, and he would have rubbed Vicks on my chest, and he would have kept Gideon away from me, and he would have worried.

"What is the capital of New Jersey?"

I had no idea. I didn't say anything.

"Dave is a thinker," Mr. Gluck said. "We'll wait while he thinks."

No one laughed or even paid attention. The boy next to me stopped coughing gradually.

"Jersey City?"

Mr. Gluck groaned. "They give me complete idiots. It's a task for a wizard, not a teacher." He walked to a spot two rows in front of me where a pair of twins whispered across the aisle to each other. Holding one of them by the ear, Mr. Gluck returned to the front of the room and went on with his speech about what dopes we were. The twin with the captured ear crossed his eyes and tried to touch his nose with his tongue.

I wasn't about to stand for hours, waiting for the teacher to give me permission to sit. I sat and opened my desk. Inside were a notebook, a bottle of ink, a pen, a pencil, and three textbooks. Gideon would have pulled out the textbooks and started memorizing them. I took the notebook and the pen and ink. I wanted to try drawing violins and see if there was something special about doing it.

A boy in the first row raised his hand. When Mr. Gluck called on him, he said, "I need the toilet."

Mr. Gluck nodded and pointed at the boy next to the one who said he had to go. "Louis, you're monitor."

They left the room. Facing away from Mr. Gluck, they were both grinning.

I started to draw, but the jumpy kid turned to me and whispered, "I'm Mike, buddy." He held out his hand to shake. The hand was speckled with ink, and some of it was still wet.

So what? I shook. "I'm Dave."

"Welcome to the HHB."

I guess I looked puzzled.

"HHB. Hebrew Home for Boys. HHB. Hell Hole for Brats."

CHAPTER 6

$\mathcal{M}$IKE WENT BACK to drawing violins. I began to draw too, but the boy who had been coughing stuck out his hand for me to shake.

"I'm Alfie, buddy," he whispered. His cheeks were flushed, like he had a fever. The cough and the fever—consumption.

I shook. "Hi."

The boy behind me tapped me on the shoulder. "I'm Eli, buddy," he said. "It's Trenton." He held his hand out too.

I shook it. "What's Trenton?"

He grinned. "The capital of New Jersey. But Mr. Cluck won't ever teach it."

Mr. Cluck. That was a good one.

The boy on Eli's right wanted to shake too. His name was Harvey, buddy. The boy on Eli's left was

Joey, buddy. In front of me were Ira, buddy, Danny, buddy, and Reuben, buddy. Maybe I should stay at the orphanage, I thought. Kids sure were friendly here, and they sure liked to call people buddy.

Mr. Cluck was still droning on about how hard he worked trying to teach us. I began to count the boys in the room. I got up to thirty-two with one row to go when a bell rang. Mr. Cluck let go of the twin's ear and dismissed us. The two boys who'd gone to the toilet had never come back.

I left with Mike, Harvey, Eli, and Alfie. I hoped it was lunchtime. I was starving.

"Did you meet Mr. Doom yet?" Mike asked, scratching his neck with one hand and slapping his thigh with the other.

"Who?"

"The superintendent. Mr. Bloom—Mr. Doom."

"Not *my* doom. I can take care of myself." He could be Doom or he could be Death, it didn't matter.

Mike laughed. He had a kind of choking laugh, like the laugh was stuck in his throat. "Buddy, you better hope so."

Alfie started coughing again. Harvey pounded him on the back.

Eli said, "You'll give him a backache on top of a cough."

Couldn't they tell Alfie had consumption? This time next year he'd probably be dead, like my friend Morty, who died during the summer after third grade.

Alfie waved his hands in front of his face. He was smaller and skinnier than me. His ears were enormous and stuck out from his head like cup handles. They were flushed too, like his face.

"You're supposed to pound a buddy when he coughs, buddy." Harvey had a hoarse voice. He was my height, but blocky-looking, like someone had carved him out with a wide chisel and hadn't bothered to finish him off with sandpaper.

Eli was tall and skinny. He had wires on his teeth. I'd never seen anything like it. Were they supposed to keep his teeth from falling out?

Mike was hard to see because he was always moving. He had straight brown hair that flew around his head and a long narrow nose.

We turned into the stairwell at the end of the corridor and started downstairs to the basement.

Harvey said, "So, Dave, buddy, are you a half or a whole?"

"Do I look like half of anything?"

"He means, is one of your parents dead or both?" Mike was hopping down the stairs backwards.

I didn't get it. "Some kids still have a mama or a papa? What are they doing here?"

Mike missed a step and almost crashed down the stairs.

"My mama's coming for me soon, buddy," Harvey said. "She's just in a jam right now. So both of yours are dead. You're a whole."

"Three-quarters. My stepmother gave me up."

"Three-quarters!" Mike said. "I like that. I'm three-quarters too then, because my grandfather's alive."

"There's no such thing as three-quarters, buddy," Harvey said. "You're both wholes."

"Who are you to decide?" I said.

"I'm me, buddy, and I'm telling you there's no such thing as a three-quarter orphan."

"Oh, yeah?" I could beat him up.

"Fight later," Eli said. "Not here."

Mike opened the door to the basement. Inside, long tables and benches were set up, with pipes overhead and pillars separating the rows of tables. The noise of a million boys yelling rang off the pipes and the low ceiling. A few grown-ups stood around. Mr. Meltzer was there, but I didn't see Mr. Doom.

We sat at an empty table. I wound up on a bench between Mike and Eli, across from the twins from our class. Harvey was at the end of the bench, with a lot of elevens between us, which was good. Each twin reached across the table to shake my hand. They shouted that their names were Jeff and Fred. Except for Fred's chipped front tooth, they looked exactly alike—red hair, freckles, dark-blue eyes.

Women started coming through a swinging door a few yards away. Each of them carried a huge, steaming pan. I smelled something like burnt rubber.

A bunch of older boys came to our table, and one sat next to each of us elevens. We had to scoot over to make room for them. Harvey got pushed off the bench. He didn't tell these big guys that he was one himself and they should shove over. He just went to another table. It couldn't have happened to a nicer guy.

"Hi," I yelled to the boy next to me. I stuck out my hand. "I'm Dave, buddy."

He didn't shake. "You're new," he said. He was almost as tall as Mr. Meltzer, and more solid. He was bigger than the other older boys by a good three inches in every direction.

"That's Moe," Mike said. "He's not your buddy. He's your bully." He pointed to the boy on his left. "He's mine. Lucky you. You got the biggest, scariest bully in the HHB."

"So what?" I could outrun him, anyway.

Mike shook his head and shrugged twice. "You'll see."

Eli added, poking his head around his bully, "And when you see, buddy, don't do anything stupid."

He had no business bossing me around. Him and Harvey.

A woman came to our table with one of the pans.

"That's the coffin," Mike said, pointing at it.

She lowered it to serve us, and I saw what was inside. Stew, noodles, and a greenish-brownish vegetable. The portion spooned onto my plate was small. I started eating. The meat was gristly. The vegetable was burnt weeds.

Next to me, Moe reached under his shirt and pulled

out a rabbit's foot on a string. He kissed the foot. Then he picked up his fork.

It went the wrong way, to my plate instead of his, and he started eating my food. The bully next to Mike was eating Mike's lunch. For a second I just stared, and in that second half my meal was gone. We ate the rest together. The only time Moe left my food alone was when a grown-up walked by.

When my plate was clean, Moe started on his own. I moved my fork to his plate too. Fair is fair. When my fork touched Moe's plate, I saw Fred nudge his brother to watch.

"Don't." Moe moved my hand away from his food. Then he put his hand down on mine and ground my palm into the tabletop. I bit my lip to keep from screaming. Under the table I kicked him as hard as I could. He didn't seem to notice. When he let go of me, my hand felt numb. Then it stung and ached. I looked at my palm. Lines from the wood grain were pressed into my skin, and I had a splinter.

I wasn't hungry anymore. I gathered a big gob of saliva in my mouth and spat onto Moe's food.

"You can spit all you want," he said with a mouth full of food. His shoulders heaved. He was laughing. "I'll eat your spit too."

I wanted to kill him and Mike's bully and Eli's and Fred's and Jeff's and all the rest of them.

"HHB, buddy," Mike said. "Happy House of Bullies."

A lady came with a basket filled with rolls. She put

one on my plate and one on Moe's. As she passed by, a roll tumbled out of the basket. At least ten hands reached, and our bench almost went over. Moe got the roll.

"You brought me luck," he told me, grabbing the piece of my roll that I hadn't stuffed in my mouth yet. Then he stood up and signaled to the other bullies at our table. They all followed him out of the dining hall.

I turned to Mike. "Why does he kiss the rabbit's foot?"

Mike did his choking laugh again. "He's superstitious. He won't step on a crack. He goes through doors sideways. When we have prayers, he stands on his left foot."

That was good to know. He was scared of something.

In the afternoon, Mr. Cluck started teaching us how to divide fractions, which I already knew. But when Alfie couldn't answer a question, he went back to his speech about what good-for-nothings we were.

I started thinking about what it would be like to live here if I stayed. I'd have to find a way to stop the bullies from taking my food. I couldn't starve. Not while Gideon was eating roast chicken and noodle pie in Chicago.

The door opened. Everybody got quiet.

It was Mr. Meltzer holding a handful of letters. "Feldman," he barked. "Karp, Silver . . ."

Mike jumped up, dropping his pen and his note-book on the floor. He rushed to the front of the room without bothering to pick them up.

" . . . Zweben, Belsky, Pincus . . ."

All over the room, boys hurried to get their mail.

". . . Elishowitz, Caros, Jacobson . . ."

Did he really say my name? Who would write to me? I just got here. I stood. I was going to feel ridiculous when I got up there if he hadn't said my name, if I'd only imagined it.

He handed me a letter. The address was in Gideon's handwriting. I shoved it into my knickers pocket. I didn't care what it said, unless it said he hadn't gone to Chicago. I pulled it out. The postmark was Chicago. I put it away again.

Mike hunched over his letter. When he finished reading, he lifted the top of his desk and dropped it in. He drummed on the desktop, then opened it again and pushed the letter in deeper.

Mr. Cluck never got back to the lesson on fractions. Except for five minutes when he gave us homework, he spent the rest of the afternoon talking about how hard it was to teach us. I don't think anybody listened, even though the horsing around had stopped. A few kids kept unfolding their letters to reread them. But most kids seemed gloomy whether or not they'd gotten any mail. One boy put his head down on the desk, and another one stared at the floor and cried.

■ ■ ■

At supper Moe and his henchmen sat with us again. After Moe kissed his rabbit's foot, he started on my food. He got less than at lunch, though. I loaded my fork, dumped the food into my mouth, swallowed without chewing, and dug back in. I got more that way, and I didn't have to taste what I was eating.

When I finished, I looked around. Everyone ate the same way I had. HHB table manners. Shovel manners.

A minute or two after my last swallow, I had to go to the toilet. The delicious food had made me sick. I hoped there was a toilet down here. Mike pointed, and I ran.

It was far away, halfway across the basement. They should have built it closer if they were going to serve food like this.

When I unbuttoned my knickers, Gideon's letter fell on the floor. I left it there while I used the toilet. Afterwards, I sat down on the toilet seat and opened the letter.

Dear Dave,

We reached Chicago on Friday, and on Saturday a letter came from Aunt Sarah. She wrote that Ida had said she was going to take you to the Hebrew Home for Boys. That's how I know where you are. Aunt Sarah says it's a decent place, where you'll get a good education.

That was a laugh.

Papa would want you to study hard for your future. I hope you won't let your mischief get in the way.

Try and stop me.

Uncle Jack and I are boarders in a house owned by a lady named Mrs. Roth. It's clean, and the food is all right. Tomorrow, I start school. I hope it's as good as yours and that some of my schoolmates are interested in more than stickball.

That's all Gideon thought I was interested in. And that's why he was glad to leave me behind.

I guess you wanted me to tell Uncle Jack that I wouldn't go to Chicago without you, but what good would it do for both of us to be in an orphanage? I'm not the kind of brother who could beat up bullies for you, so you're just as well off without me.

Better off. I was better off without him.

Uncle Jack's headaches are very bad. I keep telling him that you would be as quiet as I am. I hope he'll change his mind soon and send for you. If he does, you can't bounce balls or snap your fingers or yell or do anything noisy.

I knew that. I could be quiet.

*Please write and tell me what the orphanage is
like and what you're studying. I'll write again soon.
No matter what you think, I still care about you.*

> *Yours truly,*
> *Gideon*

I tore the letter into tiny pieces and flushed it away.

CHAPTER 7

ON MY WAY back from the toilet, I looked around. The basement was mostly open space interrupted by pillars. There were a few rooms, though. The first one I passed was full of broken furniture—desks, chairs, tables. Beyond that was a big closet. Its door was open, and I saw shelves of supplies and tools. Then, in the open space again, clotheslines were strung between the pillars, and I saw enormous sinks and wringers.

Somebody was singing. I passed a door to a small room. Inside, a man was changing his shirt and singing a sad song. I heard the words, "Please, Mr. Policeman, help me find . . ."

It looked like the man lived down here. There was a cot and a dresser. The janitor, I guessed.

Beyond the janitor's room was the furnace and the coal chute, and then I was back in the dining hall.

Everybody was leaving. I got my notebook and arithmetic textbook from our bench and followed the crowd to an auditorium, where we were supposed to do our homework. I was in the middle of a bunch of younger kids. Most of the elevens were a few rows behind me. Mike's head was down. He was probably drawing violins. The other elevens were whispering and watching out for prefects. I opened my notebook in my lap and started drawing. I tried to draw Mr. Doom's face, but he kept looking like a baby wearing spectacles, because of his wide cheeks and little piggy nose.

While I drew, I wondered what we were supposed to do when the next bell rang. They rang a bell here whenever they wanted you to do something—go to your classroom, leave your classroom, go to the dining room to have your food stolen.

I gave up on Mr. Doom. Nobody would want to look at a picture of him anyway. I started a letter.

Dear Papa,
    You'll never guess where I am. In an

I crossed out the words. If I kept writing, I'd start bawling in front of everybody. I opened my book to our homework. Dividing fractions. I could do it in my sleep.

The bell rang. I followed everybody again. I saw Mike turn and look for me. I yelled to him to wait, but he was too far ahead to hear. In the hall, some kids went into the stairwell at the end of the corridor. Some stood around talking. But most were heading toward the back of the Home. I went along.

Halfway down the back hallway, we turned into a short hall leading to a courtyard surrounded on all four sides by the HHB. There were streetlamps in each corner, which were on. Way above, the stars were out.

As soon as they got outside, everybody went crazy—running, kicking, punching, yelling, jumping. A few adults, probably prefects, stood in the far corner, talking to each other. I backed out. If we could do whatever we wanted, I wanted to find my suitcase and check out where I was supposed to sleep.

The orphanage was shaped like a square doughnut around the courtyard I'd just left. Classrooms and offices seemed to be on the main floor. I'd try the second floor, then the third.

Upstairs, I opened the first door I came to. Inside was an ocean of beds, rows and rows of them, with a suitcase under every one. A pair of slippers sat on the floor next to each bed. I'd never worn slippers in my life. The ones in here were too small for an eleven-year-old unless he was a midget.

Across from me were three tall windows. The glass in one of them was cracked, held in place with black tape. A table stood in the corner to my left, near the windows. The long wall behind me was lined with wooden cubbies.

The corner of a photograph stuck out from under the pillow on the bed closest to me. I lifted the pillow and saw a photo of a family—a girl about seven years old and an even younger girl, a man with a mustache, and a lady holding a baby. I put the pillow back and went on to the next room.

The slippers in there were even smaller. I kept going. I was checking the eighth room when the bell rang. I didn't pay attention. The slippers in the ninth room seemed about my size. I looked under the beds for my suitcase. I was walking along the third row of beds when the door opened, and the elevens came in, followed by Mr. Meltzer.

I called to him, "Where's my suitcase?"

He ignored me. I started toward him.

"It's here," a voice called from halfway across the room, near the door. It was Mike, waving and hopping.

My suitcase was under the bed next to his. Mike was half undressed. All over the room kids were changing into striped pajamas, like a prison uniform. I'd never worn pajamas. Mine were spread out on top of my bed. I put them on. The cloth wasn't much softer than my iron knickers.

I wanted to show Papa's carving to Mike so I pulled out my suitcase. It felt too light. I fumbled with the clasp.

It was empty.

Mike said something. I didn't hear what. Mr. Meltzer was sitting across the room at a table by the windows.

I ran to him. "Who took my property?" I yelled.

He took his time answering. Finally he said, "Your things belong to the Home. Mr. Doo— Mr. Bloom's orders." He barked a laugh. "Complain to him."

All right, I would. I started for the door.

Mr. Meltzer called after me, "Twenty minutes to lights-out. Be here. Or else."

Mike followed me.

In the hall, I wheeled on him. "What do you want?"

He rubbed the top of his head and scratched one foot with the other. "They throw your old clothes away, buddy. By the time you leave here, they won't fit you anymore anyway."

"I don't care about my clothes. It's something else." I had to get Papa's carving back.

"When I came, I had a *Farmer's Almanac*. They put it in the library."

"It isn't a book."

"There's other stuff too. There's a wooden sail—"

"Where's the library?"

"Come on." He led me to one of the stairwells. Two boys chasing a third ran past us. We started downstairs. Mike kept on talking. "The people who run this place are rich, so why do they take our stuff? They think they're going to open a suitcase and find a million dollars?" He did his strangled laugh again. "A boy has a million dollars. He could live at the Waldorf, but he'd rather freeze to death at the Hopeless House of Beggars."

I wasn't paying attention to Mike. I only cared about the carving.

He opened the door to the main floor. We were in the back hallway. We walked a few steps, then Mike opened a door and turned on a light switch. The walls were lined with bookcases, and there were more bookcases in the middle of the room.

"Where . . ."

Mike pointed at a glass cabinet between two windows. I went to it. It held a wooden boat, a stuffed sparrow, and shelves full of funny-looking clay animals that must have been made by kids. No carving.

"It's not here." We left the library.

Mr. Doom had said only bad boys saw his office again. Well, I was going back there. I'd grab the yardstick before he did.

"Are you really going to Mr. Doom?"

"You don't have to come."

"I'm coming. This I have to see."

I hurried down the hall.

"I don't think you should bother Mr. Doom," Mike said from behind me. "You should have seen what he did to Leon."

"Shut up. He's not going to do anything to me." But I was scared, a little anyway.

"I'll get the nurse if you need her, buddy."

The bell rang for lights out. I knocked on the door to Mr. Doom's office.

Mike hopped up and down, ready to run. "Let's go. He isn't there."

I knocked louder.

"Come on, Dave. He must have gone home. He doesn't live here."

I pounded on the door, and while I pounded I made my decision. I wasn't staying in a place that stole your private possessions. I'd get my carving back, and then I'd scram.

No answer. I turned the knob. The door was locked. I didn't know where else to look. For now.

"It's a good thing Mr. Meltzer never hits," Mike said as we ran back.

Mr. Meltzer was waiting outside our room. "Stinking brats. I told you to get back here." He herded us in ahead of him. "Get into bed. Go to sleep."

Mr. Meltzer left, and all the elevens crowded around my bed.

"Did you find Mr. Doom?" one of them asked. It was too dark to see who was talking.

"If he did, he'd be on a stretcher," another voice said. I think it was Harvey. The voice sounded hoarse.

"He wasn't there," I said.

"He pounded on his office door," Mike said, bragging about me, "like Mr. Doom should be scared of him."

"Remember when Leon told Mr. Doom the food was lousy?" said Alfie, the kid with the cough. My eyes were getting used to the dark.

Somebody tall said, "What happened, buddy?"

"Mr. Doom whacked him so hard he flew ten feet."

"And bounced twice." That was one of the twins.

They started telling Mr. Doom stories. I stretched out on my bed and closed my eyes, but I heard every word. Mr. Doom's victims lost teeth, needed stitches, needed crutches. Sixteen-year-old bullies begged for mercy, screamed for their mamas.

Finally the buddies drifted back to their beds, and gradually the feeling in the room changed as they fell asleep. I heard snoring. Someone whimpered. Someone coughed. The room was so big it was almost like sleeping outside. And it was so cold and humid that sleet could have started coming down. One blanket wasn't enough. I put my pillow over my head to block out everyone's noise and to keep my ears warm.

I swore an oath, whispering into the thin mattress. I would take back the carving and get out of here.

CHAPTER 8

I COULDN'T SLEEP. Mike was as jerky in his sleep as he was awake. One of his bed's legs was shorter than the others, and the bed was dancing. It made such a racket I didn't know how anybody could sleep. I stood up. Maybe I could prowl around and find the carving.

Daredevil Dave was at it again.

I tiptoed to the door, holding my slippers. Outside I blinked in the light of the hall. Two doors away from me, at the end of the corridor, Mr. Meltzer sat in a chair. I got ready to say I had to go to the toilet, but he didn't move, and I realized he was asleep.

I put on my slippers and walked a few steps. He still didn't move. I clapped my hands softly. He shifted in his chair and started snoring. I headed for the stairwell at the opposite end of the corridor, walking fast, but quietly.

The door to the stairwell creaked. I looked back, frightened. He was still asleep. I closed the door gently behind me and let out a deep breath. There was no light on the stairs. I took my slippers off again and felt my way down, hanging on to the banister.

I wondered if any prefects were prowling around. If I was caught, I'd say, "Where am I? Where's Ida? Why am I in an icebox?" They'd think I was sleepwalking. At least I hoped they would.

The first floor was dark, but I was used to it by now. I stood still, listening. My stomach rumbled. It sounded loud enough to wake Mr. Meltzer. The corner of the corridor showed ahead, a deeper black than the rest of the gloom. Touching the wall as I went, I edged along.

I didn't know the asylum well enough to guess where they'd put a carving. I came to a door and turned the knob. Locked. The next one was too. All the doors on both sides of the corridor were locked. Even the library was locked now.

At the end of the hall, it was a little less dark. I pictured Mr. Doom in the lobby, holding his yardstick, waiting to ambush roving boys.

I glided along, as quiet as snow. Till I stepped on a loose tile. *Clink*. Not loud, but it echoed in the hall and pounded in my ears.

Should I run? No. Running would make more noise. I flattened myself against the wall. I heard a bong and flew two feet straight up. I dropped a slipper.

It was the clock outside, over the entrance. It had struck during the day, but it hadn't sounded so loud. There were lots of bongs. Eleven o'clock. I tiptoed to the end of the hall and turned the corner.

The corridor was empty, and the lobby looked empty too. I checked the office doors on the way to the front door, but they were all locked. The front door was locked too, only the lock was on my side for a change. I guessed it was to keep burglars out. I was surprised there wasn't another one to keep us in.

The lock turned. I swung the door open and stepped outside. Out of the Home.

It was slightly warmer out here. There was a breeze, and clouds raced across the moon. I breathed in deeply. The air was fresh and clean. Maybe I should forget the carving, just leave and never come back.

But I couldn't forget it.

I could leave, though, and come back before anybody woke up. I grinned, thinking of all the rules I'd be breaking. I walked to the gate, swinging my arms.

When I got there I saw why it had been easy to open the front door. The gate to the wrought-iron fence that circled the HHB was locked, and you needed a key to open it.

I pushed through the bushes that grew against the fence to see if I could squeeze between the posts, but they were too close together. And the crossbar was too high for me to reach.

I was a prisoner.

On the 136th Street side of the HHB, there was a smaller gate. It was locked too, but an oak tree grew nearby, and a big branch stretched over into the land of the free.

The lowest branch was beyond my reach, but the trunk had a crack about three feet up that I could fit my foot in. I tucked my slippers into the waist of my pajamas. Then I stepped into the crack and launched myself at the lowest branch. I fell three times, but I made it on the fourth try.

From my perch in the tree I looked around. All the lights were out in the Home. The street outside was quiet. I climbed up to the branch that hung over the fence. From there I stepped onto the fence's crossbar. Then it was easy. I slid down the fence.

I didn't know the neighborhood. I'd only seen Broadway and Amsterdam Avenue. Broadway was too busy, so I went the other way, toward Amsterdam Avenue.

I stood on the HHB side of Amsterdam and 136th Street. Across Amsterdam was a concrete wall, hiding who-knew-what. I crossed and walked along 136th Street next to the wall. No one was out here with me.

The concrete wall ended halfway down the block, and I found out what was behind it: a huge stadium, with rows and rows of empty seats. I waved to the seats. I took a bow. Orphan escapes from Hated Home for Boys. Hurrah! I bowed again.

Across the next street—Convent Avenue—was a vacant lot with brown weeds up to my waist and no sidewalk. I pushed through to the next avenue, Saint Nicholas Terrace, where a woodsy park sloped down steeply in front of me. Beyond it, streetlights and lighted windows twinkled.

Papa would not want me to go into that park. He wouldn't want me to be out here at all. He'd want me and Gideon to be sharing our old couch, with Ida in the next room. And he'd like to be there too, alive. I swallowed. He wasn't getting anything he wanted.

I climbed over a low wall and stepped into the park. The wind ruffled the leaves that were still on the trees. Dead leaves crackled under my feet. When I got Papa's carving back, I could build a place to live in here. As I walked, I looked for good hideouts. I saw an out-cropping of rock. There might be a cave. I'd be a hermit. I'd set traps for mice and squirrels, and I'd roast them over the fire I made. I'd get a chisel from somewhere and teach myself to make carvings like Papa did. I'd live in the park by day, but at night I'd roam. I'd break into the HHB and set the elevens free. We'd live together like Robin Hood and his merry band.

The street was now only a few yards away. A car's headlamps flashed by. I hid behind a tree. Another car went by, and another. There was a lot of traffic here. Somebody might see me and call the police. Somebody might kidnap me.

Voices called out. I heard the tinkle of a piano.

I crept to a shoulder-high boulder and ducked behind it. Another car drove by. And another. This one stopped.

Had someone seen me?

A car door slammed. "Come back at three, Robert," a man's voice said.

I peeked around the boulder. A redheaded man leaned into the window of a chauffeured Pierce-Arrow. A lady waited for him, standing under the streetlight. I wished I could get a close-up look at the car, but it drove away. The man and the lady were all dressed up. The lady's hat, which was shaped like an upside-down fishbowl, came down so low it covered her eyebrows. The man took her arm, and they went into the apartment building on the corner.

Four cars were parked at the curb. One of them was a Peerless. I couldn't believe it—a Peerless. I had to go look at it.

No one was on the street. The piano started up again, coming from the building on the corner. I heard laughter. I stepped out and ran across the street.

CHAPTER
9

THE CAR GLEAMED, without a speck of dirt or mud. I peered through the driver's window. The dashboard was mahogany. Papa wouldn't believe it. It must have weighed a ton and cost a fortune. The speedometer went up to eighty miles an hour. I wondered what it would feel like to go that fast. There was an altimeter, so if you drove up a mountain you'd know how high you were. The gauges were edged in silver. It had an automatic starter—all the classy cars did.

There was more mahogany around the windows, and a mahogany rail to hang on to, and a—

I heard footsteps and men's voices. I crouched behind the car. Somebody wailed. No, not somebody— some thing. It was the strangest sound I ever heard. It seemed to be laughing.

I peeked over the hood. A colored man playing

a trumpet—a laughing trumpet—was walking back-wards around the corner at the far end of the block. Another colored man was following him, clapping out a beat.

The door of the building on the corner opened, the same building the couple had gone into. A colored lady came out and hollered, "Hush, Martin, you'll wake the neighbors."

The trumpeter stopped playing and hollered back, "Your neighbors are fools to sleep when they could be stepping."

The other man yelled, "I told him to be still. I shouted 'Be still' at least three times, but no matter how loud I hollered, he wouldn't pay me any mind."

The three of them laughed. The men went to the woman and each of them kissed her on the cheek. Then they went inside. I stood up. This sure was different from my old neighborhood.

I looked up at the building, which was seven stories tall, made of cream-colored brick. A stone pedestal sat on either side of the door, and on top of each pedestal, dark green ivy grew out of a big stone urn.

On the third floor the lights were on. I saw shapes against the half-open windows—a woman with her arms raised, a man smoking a long cigarette, two people talking.

A piece of paper wafted out of one of the windows. As it drifted down, I saw that it was a dollar. I grabbed it before it touched the ground. Then I ran back to the park and hid. Somebody was going to come after the dollar.

But nobody came out. Upstairs, a trumpet now blared along with the tinkling piano. My stomach growled. They were a bunch of rich people if they didn't care about a dollar.

I tucked the money into the toe of my slipper and crossed the street again. I stood looking up at the building. Maybe they'd toss more money out. I wondered if there was any food in there. Meatballs. My mouth watered. Chicken. Lamb—

"So, nu? Are you going to return the money?" The voice came from behind me.

I ran.

"Get him," the voice said.

There were two of them! Or more.

Wings beat at me. A bird! It kept crashing into my face. I put my arm up to knock it away. It squawked, "Gozlin! Holdupnik!"

Somebody grabbed my arm. "So you're a thief and—"

"Make your bird—"

"Enough already, Bandit," the human voice said. "I got him."

The bird stopped batting at me.

"I don't have any money." I turned to see who held me.

An old white man with a long gray beard. I squirmed, but he was strong. I couldn't get away. The bird, a big gray parrot, perched on his shoulder and squawked, "Tell for you your fortune?"

"Not yet, Bandit," the old man said.

"I don't have any money," I repeated. My stomach rumbled loudly.

"You think I'm stupid? It's in your slipper. Should I look?" He started to bend while still holding me.

"No. Don't look."

He straightened up. "All right, I won't. We'll just go inside and you'll give it back."

If I gave back this dollar, maybe I could stay awhile and pick up a few more. But how could I go inside dressed the way I was? "In pajamas?" I said.

He stood back and looked me over.

The parrot squawked again, "Tell for you your fortune?"

He let go of me and unknotted his tie, which had orange polka dots on a bright green background. He tied it around my neck. "Now you could go anywhere. And I look better too. The tie was pretentious."

I didn't know what he was talking about. His black suit sagged all over, and his beard could have belonged to Rip Van Winkle. His face sagged too, with bags under his eyes and drooping wrinkled skin on his cheeks. Tie or no tie, he was shabby.

"So, boychik, what's your name? I should know my own grandson's name."

Why would he pretend I was his grandson? I

didn't answer. My stomach growled again.

"You're hungry, boychik? There's plenty of food upstairs."

The parrot squawked, "Boychik."

"Dave Rubino," I said, borrowing our old boarders' last name. I wanted this adventure to keep going. It was like a dream—a parrot in my face, a Peerless, pajamas and a tie.

"Pleased to make your acquaintance. I'm Solomon Gruber. Solly the gonif." He held out his hand for me to shake.

We shook. I wondered what a gonif was. I knew it was a Yiddish word. You couldn't live in my neighborhood and not recognize Yiddish. I knew a few words. I knew what a boychik was—a little boy. But we were Sephardic Jews. We didn't come from the places where people spoke Yiddish, like Russia and Germany. Papa spoke Spanish and Turkish and English and Ladino, which is a mixture of Spanish and Hebrew. I only spoke English.

We went up three stone steps to get into the building. "Hey, Solly," the elevator man called as we came through the door.

"Shalom, your honor," Solly said. "Who's on the piano?"

"Jake."

"Good."

We stepped into the elevator. There was a flowered

carpet, and the walls were red. The elevator man closed the brass gate. We rose, and I watched the second floor go by.

The parrot squawked, "In the cards. In the cards."

The elevator man got out with us on the third floor. The music was louder here. The hall was filled with furniture—a dresser, a bed, a table, a couch, even a huge cactus. We had to pick our way around everything to get to the door of the apartment the noise was coming from.

"Who's the boy, Solly?" A colored lady sat at a table outside the apartment. On the table was a glass bowl half filled with change. Twenty dollars or more. A fortune.

"My grandson. Dave Rubino, meet Mary Lou Barnes. Dave has the power, just like me. Not like his parents, the alrightniks."

Alrightniks? Power?

She smiled. "Pleased to meet you. Pretty tie."

"Thank you, Miss Barnes." I blushed, feeling silly in pajamas and a tie.

"Ante up, Solly."

"Ante up," the parrot squawked.

He took a quarter out of his pocket and dropped it in the bowl.

"Your grandson, Solly."

"He's only six."

"If he's six, then I'm a mackerel. Pay up. It's a good crowd. You'll make plenty tonight."

That meant he worked here. I didn't understand.

"Okay, okay. I'm paying." He put more money in the bowl. "And here's a nickel for the boychik's dinner. He's hungry."

Wait. What about me giving back the dollar?

"Come," Solly said. "Show them you have the power."

CHAPTER
10

I FOLLOWED SOLLY through the open door into a big room filled with grown-ups but no furniture, just some chairs pushed against the wall. Most of the people were colored, but a few were white. The red-headed man who'd come in the Pierce-Arrow was standing near me.

I stood still, staring.

The air was full of perfume. If I stuck out my tongue, I'd taste it. Everyone was dressed up. Some of the men's suits were surprising colors, like light blue or dark yellow. And some of their trousers were crazily wide. You could make two pairs of pants out of that much cloth. The women's dresses were the opposite— not enough cloth. They only covered the ladies' legs down to their knees.

The lady closest to me had a fox fur wrapped

around her shoulders, even though it was hot in here. I knew it was fox because the head was right there, under her chin, and the little feet hung down on her chest.

Everybody seemed happy. They reminded me of Papa and his brothers and sisters when they used to get together.

"Nice, isn't it, boychik?" Solly had to shout for me to hear him. Everybody else was yelling, and underneath the voices was the hum of music coming from somewhere deeper in the apartment.

I nodded.

"I wish my grandfather took me to a rent party when I was your age. Not that there were any."

"What's a rent party?"

"In Harlem if you can't pay the rent you have a party. The quarter everybody paid to get in, that will be the rent."

If only Ida had known!

"What did you mean before when you said I had 'the power'?"

He ignored the question. "First a little pleasure, then a little business. You'll eat and I'll listen to the music. Then we'll work."

I didn't ask about the dollar. I didn't want to remind him of it.

He grabbed my arm. "Boychik, are you a landsman?"

"What's a lontsmon, Mr. Gruber?"

"Call me Grandpa. If you don't know, you aren't."

He paused. "Dave Rubino. . . . Could be Sephardic. A landsman is a fellow Jew."

"I'm Sephardic."

"Then don't eat the meat. It might be pork. If you're kosher, don't eat anything." He patted my cheek. "Have fun, boychik." He pushed his way through the crowd to a doorway at the end of the room.

All around me people were eating and talking. The food was on a table against the wall. I pushed through the crowd. At home, we weren't kosher. But even if I was, I might have eaten anyway. This was food that smelled like food. I loaded my plate with chicken, potato salad, cole slaw, rice and beans, and bread.

I ate standing up, facing the wall across the table. The wallpaper was pale green leaves with big pale violet flowers. I stared at it, my mind on what was in my mouth. The chicken was the best—peppery and juicy. When I finished eating two loaded plates, I poured myself a glass of water from a white china pitcher.

"Don't drink that, pajama boy, if you want to live."

I turned around. A colored girl about my age smiled at me like I was the newest thing in the world. New, and she was glad I'd come along.

"Uhhh," I said.

She laughed. "Don't drink it. They pretend it's gin, but they put in kerosene and a lot of other junk."

Kerosene! I put the glass down. "I thought it was water." Without thinking, I added, "You look like a flower." It was the way she stood—straight with her head tilted up, a skinny stem holding up a beautiful face.

"A flower would wear a green dress. This is blue." She laughed again.

I shrugged, embarrassed at what I'd said.

"Do you want some water?"

"Uh-huh."

"Come with me." She took my hand. "Bring your glass." I picked the glass up with my other hand, and she pulled me through the crowd.

Her hand was smaller than mine. I didn't want to crush it, but I didn't want to hold it so loosely that we got separated. Was I holding it too hard or too soft? I tried to keep the pressure steady, and my hand ached from the effort.

As we moved through the room, people kept calling out to her.

"That young Irma Lee sure looks pretty."

"I swear that child is going to break some hearts."

"Hey, Irma Lee! Where's your mama, girl?"

She answered the last one. "Somewhere, gabbing."

We entered a long, narrow hall that was also crowded. This was the biggest apartment I'd ever seen. We passed a closed door. Irma Lee cocked her head at it. "Poker. Craps."

As we went farther along, the music got louder. The drum played by itself for a minute. I found myself walking to the beat. We turned into a short hall with doors on the right and the left. Irma Lee pulled me into the left-hand door and then let go of my hand.

We were in the kitchen. Two women sat at the table. I smiled at them, wishing again that I wasn't in pajamas. Irma Lee ignored them. I heard her mutter, "Darn!" She rinsed my glass, and I noticed there were two faucets. This apartment got hot water, not just cold. I looked around. There was a gas stove, not coal, and the icebox was three times the size of ours at home. No wonder they had to throw a party to pay the rent. It was probably ten times what Papa used to pay.

Outside the kitchen, the drum got softer and the other instruments joined in.

"Baby girl!" one of the ladies said. "Come to your mama."

Irma Lee looked at me for a second, and there was a message in the look, but I didn't know what it was. She filled my glass and gave it to me. Then she took my hand again and tugged me along to the table. "Yes, ma'am. Here I am."

Irma Lee's mama gathered her into a hug—except Irma Lee's arm stuck out, because her hand still held mine. "Having a fine time, baby girl?" her mama murmured into Irma Lee's hair.

I watched them while I drank the water. They didn't look alike. Irma Lee was delicate. Her mother was tall, with a broad face and large features. She was colored too, but she was lighter than Irma Lee.

"I'm not a baby, Mama." Irma Lee's voice was muffled against her mother's chest. "Let me go."

"I know you're not, baby girl." Her mama released Irma Lee, who gave herself a little shake. "Say hello to your cousin, baby—Irma Lee, and introduce us to your young friend . . ." Her eyebrows went up. ". . . in the outlandish duds."

"Mama! They're not outlandish. They're . . . uh . . . swell."

She was swell!

Irma Lee went on. "Hello, Cousin Emmie, ma'am. Thank you for inviting me to your party."

"Hello, honey," the cousin said. She was a plump woman with short hair, held away from her face by two silver barrettes.

Irma Lee couldn't introduce me because she didn't know my name. "I'm Dave Caros." Oops! I should have said Rubino, the name I'd given Solly. Or I should have said Gruber. "I'm Solly Gruber's grandson."

"Solly!" Irma Lee's mama said. "Is that old gonif here? Tell him to come say hi to Odelia."

"Yes, missus," I said.

"I'm Mrs. Packer, Irma Lee's mama."

"Can I be excused, Mama?" Irma Lee said. "I was showing Dave around."

"Go on, baby. I won't keep you," Mrs. Packer said. Then she called after us, "Don't tell him every idea that pops into your head, honey. Keep something to yourself."

"Mama!" Irma Lee pulled me out of the room. Outside, she spun around. She whispered in a rush, "She acts like I'm six. I hate when she does that. I wish she wouldn't say a single word. Not a single word." She calmed down. "Do you need to find your grand-daddy?"

I shook my head. "The old gonif will find me."

"Come on then." She led me back through the apartment and out the door to the stairs next to the elevator. We sat on the steps going up to the next floor.

"She's not my real mama," Irma Lee said. "She's my real mama's cousin. She adopted me when my real mama and my daddy died."

Irma Lee was an orphan too.

"I—" I stopped. I had almost told her I was an orphan. But I couldn't, because Solly's alrightniks—whatever they were—were supposed to be my parents. "Um, I'm sorry about your mother and father."

She shook her head and her two braids danced. "I don't remember them. I was only two. Odelia's my mama, except when she hugs me in front of people and talks too much, and some other times." She giggled. "Now how come your mama let you out of her house in your pajamas?"

I couldn't tell the truth, but I didn't want to lie either. "She doesn't know." The words were true, but I was fooling her, so it was really a lie. "Sol—Grandpa and I snuck out together. He gave me his tie to wear."

"It's . . ." She laughed. ". . . swell, like I told Mama." Then she took both my hands. "Dave Caros, don't lie to me." I stopped breathing. Did she know about the dollar? "Will you be my friend?"

CHAPTER 11

SAID YES, even though I'd probably never see her again. I *wanted* to be her friend.

"Good." She leaned back and crossed her ankles. She didn't say anything, just smiled at me.

I smiled back. We sat there for a minute or two, smiling at each other.

"Where do you live?" I could visit her when I left the asylum.

"On a Hundred and Thirty-fourth Stree—"

"Tell for you your fortune?" a parrot squawked.

"There you are, boychik." Solly poked his head into the stairwell. "With the loveliest lady at the party."

I wished he'd go away. I wanted to stay here with Irma Lee.

But she smiled happily at him. "My mama says for you to tell her hello."

"I did already. Come, Daveleh. We're not heiresses, so it's time to work."

I stood up. I couldn't let Irma Lee see I didn't know what he was talking about. And did he mean *she* was an heiress?

"Can I help, Mr. Gruber?" she said.

"No, sweetheart. They all know you. You'd be bad for business. You can see Dave later."

Irma Lee went back in to the party. Solly knelt down to straighten my tie. "You should close your eyes when I get started. Rocking back and forth is good. If you feel like making a big groan, don't be shy. But if you laugh, or do anything to spoil my business, that dollar will be out of your slipper before you can say 'gesundheit.'"

"What's your business?"

"We tell fortunes." He reached into his pocket and pulled out a deck of worn cards. "With these." He stood up.

Could he really predict the future? Did he think I could too? Was that why he'd grabbed me on the street?

"Real fortunes?"

"Real-shmeal. Do you think a deck of cards can tell the future?"

I shook my head.

"Smart boychik. Let's get started."

So that's what a gonif was. Somebody who fools people out of their money. A crook. But not an evil crook. I was a gonif too. I had taken the dollar.

"Wait. What time is it?"

"You have another engagement?" He pulled a watch out of his pocket. "Five after one. You have time for a little business?"

I nodded. I had hours. It would only take a few minutes to walk back to the Honking House of Bells. But could I climb back in? I hadn't thought about that. There had to be a way. I'd worry about it later.

"Let's begin, then." We went back into the apartment, and Solly put his arm around my shoulder. "Tell for you your fortune?" he called.

The parrot squawked, "Tell for you your fortune?"

"A quarter a card," Solly chanted.

A quarter! Just for a card! For a quarter I could buy a hot dog and a double-scoop ice cream cone and an orangeade and a chocolate bar. A delicious meal.

Solly was still chanting. "A half a dollar, a year. For a dollar, your life."

He wasn't loud enough. Everybody was yelling to each other.

"Mackey, girl, the last time I saw you—"

". . . what happened to James—"

A man tilted back his head and drank from a silver bottle.

"Honey, what's in your potato salad? I never—"

". . . fell over from that rotgut. Fell—"

"Solly!" A woman waved at us from across the room.

Solly started toward her. "A repeat customer," he told me.

"I'm so glad you're here," she said. "Everything turned out— Who's he?"

"My grandson. Dave, meet Mrs. Smith, a sweet lady."

A grandmotherly white lady in a short red dress with sequins smiled at me.

I said hello. Solly went on, "Dave has the power. He's going to help me in my old age."

Mrs. Smith said, "You were right last week. I should always listen to Solly. That's what I tell everyone."

"How many cards tonight?" Solly said. "For my best customers, two for a quarter."

"Then I'll take two. Make them count, Solly."

"Come to my office." He led us to the food table, where he moved the cole slaw to make room for his cards. Solly maneuvered so that I stood between him and Mrs. Smith.

She took a purse out of her pocketbook and handed Solly a quarter.

He tapped the deck three times. Then he noticed me watching and passed his hand down over my eyes. "Close your eyes, boychik. Better to feel the power." He told Mrs. Smith, "He has great power, but he has a lot to learn."

I kept my eyes open a slit. I couldn't miss this. Solly turned over a card. A three of clubs. The parrot squawked, "Mazel. Mazel tov."

"Is it lucky, Solly? Did the parrot say it was lucky?"

"That's what he said, but he's just a bird. What does

he know? Could be lucky. The cards never lie, but sometimes they aren't what they seem. Play it. Take a chance."

"I will. Trouble comes in threes, so why not luck?"

"Are you feeling anything, boychik?" He kicked my shin lightly as he turned over another card.

I was supposed to rock back and forth, groan if I felt like it. I rocked, but I didn't feel like groaning. Did he want me to rock slow or fast? Forwards and backwards, or side to side? I rocked slowly from side to side.

"Joker!" Mrs. Smith said. "Is that bad?"

"Impossible to tell unless I see the next card. A joker followed by a queen is very bad . . ."

Mrs. Smith opened her pocketbook again. "Two more cards, Solly."

What a racket! Every other card was probably a joker.

". . . But a joker followed by a king is good." Solly pocketed the quarter and turned over a card.

The parrot squawked, "In the cards. In the cards."

The next card was an ace of hearts. I tried a low moan.

"Why did he moan?"

"An ace," Solly said, "is the most important card in the deck. That's why he moaned. You are the ace. You are the one. In this crisis the ace must decide."

I groaned.

Mrs. Smith groaned and moaned. "Give me a beautiful card. I need a beautiful card."

It was a nine of diamonds.

"This is good. Not perfect, but good. Your crisis will turn out well."

Mrs. Smith stood on tiptoe to kiss Solly on the forehead. "You set my mind at rest."

The parrot shrieked, "Gevalt! Gevalt!"

Solly nudged me with his foot. I groaned deeply.

"If it's going to be all right, why did he groan?"

"Could be he has reservations. Could be I haven't seen all there is to see."

"He's only a child. How could he know?"

"Let me tell you about this child. A week ago I had such a pain in my side." Solly clutched his side. "I could hardly breathe. This boychik says to me, 'Grandpa, until you pay your debt, your side will hurt.' So, right then and there, I gave my cousin the dollar I owed him, and—pfft!—my side felt like it was sixteen years old. That's the power in this boychik."

What a gonif! He was good!

Mrs. Smith took another quarter out of her handkerchief. "I want him to play the next card. Not you, Solly."

Solly knelt down next to me. "Daveleh, Mrs. Smith wants you to turn over a card. Can you do it?"

I didn't know whether he wanted me to nod or not. I groaned.

"He can do it," Solly said. "Nu, I have a better idea. I'll spread out the cards and he can pick the perfect one for you. But this one card costs a quarter."

"I'll take it."

Solly spread the cards on the table. "Dave, Mrs. Smith needs your help. Can you help her?"

I groaned, like Mr. Doom was strangling me.

The parrot squawked, "Oy vay! Gevalt!"

Solly took my right hand and guided it till it was in the air over the cards. "There, boychik, pick the perfect card."

I started to pick one. Then I stopped, my hand hanging in the air. What if there was a special card he wanted me to pick?

"What's he waiting for?"

"He's waiting for the power to tell him the right card. When his hand starts to tremble, you'll know the power has come to him."

I waited a few seconds, then made my hand tremble. I threw in a groan. But I still didn't know which card to pick. My hand made circles above the cards while I waited for a signal. Then I realized that whatever I picked, Solly would know what to say. I lowered my hand and almost touched a card. Mrs. Smith breathed in sharply. Solly didn't do anything. I almost touched another card. Then I tapped one.

This was fun!

CHAPTER 12

"THANK YOU, BOYCHIK." Solly turned the card over. A king of clubs. "Ah. Now I see. The boy is brilliant."

"What does it mean? Is it bad?"

"What's a club? A club is a group of people. You need help in your crisis. You need a king, a friend. If you share your burden, all will be well. The cards have spoken. Daveleh, you can wake up now."

I rubbed my hands over my eyes like I had just woken up. "Did we help her, Grandpa? Will everything be all right?"

"Yes, little momzer, we helped her."

"Good." I smiled up at Mrs. Smith.

She beamed at me. "Thank you, son."

She didn't buy any more cards. She said good-bye, promising to rave about him and me to all her friends.

When she'd gone, Solly said, "You're a natural, boychik. I wish I really did have a grandson like you."

Maybe I could live with Solly. I could earn my keep by helping him tell fortunes.

"Where do you live?" I said.

"Why? You're planning to send me flowers?"

I didn't know how to answer. Why wouldn't he tell me?

"On Stanton Street. And you?"

He lived in my old neighborhood! "We used to live on Ludlow." I was excited. "I went to P.S. 42, on Hester Street." If I stayed with him, I could go back there.

"So, nu? Where do you live now?"

I was embarrassed. "At the HHB."

"I should know what an HHB is?"

I shrugged and shook my head.

"Never mind. We're wasting time. Tell for you your fortune?" He started walking. Bandit squawked, "Tell for you your fortune?"

I saw Irma Lee across the room. I wondered if she knew Solly told fake fortunes.

Our next customers were the couple who'd arrived in the Pierce-Arrow. They didn't believe Solly could see the future, and they laughed at everything he said. I didn't bother rocking or groaning for them.

But they gave Solly two dollars for a whole-life fortune for each of them. Solly told the man that he'd be rich someday, but I knew he must be rich already to spend two dollars on a phony fortune. Solly warned him to watch for a man with one blue eye and one green eye. He told the woman that she'd marry an English lord and have twelve children.

At the end, the man gave Solly an extra dime as a tip. In less than an hour, he'd made two dollars and eighty-five cents! It used to take Papa a whole day to earn five dollars.

"Dave!" Irma Lee pushed through the crowd to us. She was wearing a coat now. "Mama says I can invite you and Mr. Gruber to *our* party." She opened a little blue pocketbook and took out two pieces of stiff white paper. She gave one to me and one to Solly.

In script with lots of curlicues it said,

You are cordially invited to
A gathering
At the city residence of Miss Odelia Packer
143 West One Hundred Thirty-fourth Street
Saturday evening, December 11th, 1926
Come early, stay late!
Conversation, Music, Potations, and Comestibles

"Can you come?"

"Mazel tov!" the parrot squawked.

It was more than a month away. I didn't know where I'd be by then. But I'd come, no matter where I was. I nodded. "Yes." Whoa! "Can't I, Grandpa?"

"The boychik and I wouldn't miss it."

"I have to go now. 'Bye." She smiled at me and turned to leave.

"'Bye," I said.

She turned back and touched my shoulder. Then she leaned up to kiss me on the cheek. The kiss was soft and light and warm and over in a second. "'Bye," she said again.

"'Bye," I repeated.

She left, threading through the crowd. She was perfect!

"Shayneh shvartzeh maidel," Solly said.

"What does that mean?"

"Pretty black girl."

Pretty wasn't good enough, and black didn't sound right. Her skin was brown. Beautiful. Perfect.

I bent down and put the invitation in my other slipper. "What time is it?" I asked.

It was twenty after two. I still had time.

"Tell for you your fortune?" Solly chanted.

"Tell for you your fortune?" the parrot echoed.

We had three more customers. The first was a colored man who wasn't interested in picture cards or in anything Solly said. He only wanted numbers he could "play." When the card was a nine, he wrote it down. When it was a three, he wrote that down. When it was a king, he growled, "Another one." I didn't have to groan or do anything.

The numbers man left after he'd bought three cards.

Our next customer was a colored woman who was repeat business, like Mrs. Smith had been. When I groaned, she asked Solly if I was "communing with souls in the hereafter."

The last customer bought a lifetime fortune for his girlfriend. They were like the other couple—they didn't think anything Solly said would come true, they were just having fun. Solly gave them nice lives. They were going to get married in seven months, have five children, and live in a warm climate. He was going to be elected to Congress, and she was going to be in the movies. They left us laughing their heads off.

Solly's grand total was seven dollars, for an hour and a half of work. "Enough already," he said. "It's time for jazz music. Boychik, get ready for heaven."

Jazz. It didn't sound Yiddish. "What time is it?"

It was three-thirty. In an hour I should leave.

Solly led me back to the hallway Irma Lee and I had been in before. We passed the vestibule that led to the kitchen and turned into the next doorway.

The light was dim. The floor shook. All over the room people were jumping around, dancing to the happiest music I'd ever heard.

We edged our way toward the musicians. Chairs were pushed against the wall in here too. Solly sat on one and started pumping his knees, nodding, and tapping his feet in time to the music. I stood next to him, not moving, although that was hard. This music wanted you to dance.

Nobody was playing the drums right now. There were just a pianist and the man I'd seen on the street—Martin—playing the trumpet. For two people, they made a lot of music.

It was wide-awake music, nothing like the waltzes Papa used to whistle. If I could have painted it, I would have used bright colors and short straight lines. The music was the opposite of the HHB. It was warm and happy and you couldn't hold it in. This music didn't know about locks and iron fences—it would blast through anything.

I closed my eyes to hear better. Sometimes the piano was on top, and sometimes the trumpet was, and sometimes it sounded like they were talking to each other. The pianist had to have a hundred fingers to play the way he did. And it was a good thing we were in New York City, not Jericho, because with Martin playing the trumpet those walls wouldn't have stood a chance.

I opened my eyes. A man and a woman hopped in a circle with their arms over their heads. Another couple crossed and uncrossed their hands over their knees in time to the music. And another kicked and hopped at the same time. I guessed they were doing the Charleston. I'd never seen it, but I'd heard of it.

The only ones who weren't dancing were Solly and me and four men standing near the musicians, watching them. One of them nodded his head slowly, and another kept time with one hand.

The song ended. A few people clapped. Somebody

called, "Play 'Cake Walking Babies.'" Somebody else yelled, "My man, Martin." The pianist stood up and stretched. Somebody called, "Give Nate a turn. I want to hear some real music."

Solly told me, "It's a cutting contest, boychik. Each musician tries to show he plays best."

The pianist pushed back the bench and joined the men who'd been standing around. The one who took his place was the other man I'd seen on the street, the one who'd clapped while Martin played his trumpet. For a few seconds he just touched a few keys, and I thought, He doesn't know how to play—he's going to be so embarrassed.

Somebody yelled, "Do that 'Chop Suey' number."

Then the new pianist got going, and his playing was even better than the other guy's. The new man sounded like he had a *thousand* fingers. Everybody started dancing again. I felt like marching around the room and clapping and shouting. Instead, I sat next to Solly and tapped my feet.

I watched the dancers nearest us, trying to figure out how to dance like them. I moved my feet the way they did, but it didn't seem right. I'd have to stand up to really try it, but I was too shy.

The next song was slow, and the trumpet was more important than the piano. I closed my eyes. The trumpet purred and hummed, and sometimes it sang so sweetly it could have been a lullaby. I leaned my head back against the wall behind my chair. I wondered if

Irma Lee knew how to do the Charleston. I didn't know anything about dancing. But if I tried it, I knew she wouldn't laugh at me.

I'd be her friend, just like I promised I would. I'd be her friend even if I had to climb down the walls of the asylum to see her.

The music stopped. I opened my eyes. Solly was there, laughing and talking with the musicians, but everyone else was gone. I'd been asleep.

The sky outside the window was gray, not black. It was morning! Was everybody awake at the HHB? How was I going to get back in?

CHAPTER 13

SOLLY WAS TELLING the musicians, "A joker usually means I get another—"

I rushed to him. "What time is it?"

"You're awake, boychik?"

"What time is it?"

"This is your grandson, Solly?" asked Martin, the trumpeter.

"What time is it? I have to know."

"What time? What time?" the parrot squawked.

"He's late for a date," one of the musicians said. The others laughed.

Shut up, everybody. Just tell me the time.

Solly pulled out his watch. "Five-fifteen."

When did everybody wake up? When did Mr. Doom get there?

"I have to go. 'Bye." The musicians thought this

was hilarious, and they started laughing again. Then I remembered that I couldn't leave without my grand-father. "Let's go, Grandpa. Hurry."

Solly put the cards in his pocket. "Another time, gentlemen. I'll make you fortune-tellers, and you can make a musician out of me, I should be so lucky."

I tugged Solly through the apartment.

"I'm coming, boychik, I'm coming."

Hardly anyone was still here. A man was stretched out across four chairs, sleeping. Two men were moving furniture from the hall back into the apartment.

When we got downstairs, I said, " 'Bye. I have to go." If only I could fly—to the HHB and then in a window.

"Not so fast. What kind of grandpa am I if I don't deliver you to your HHB safe and sound?"

"I'll be safe," I said. I couldn't stand here talking.

"Then maybe *I* need protection. Which way do we go?"

I pointed at the park. "On the other side of that."

"Oy! I'll trip on a root, it'll be the end of me. Suppose we go around."

It would take too long. "I'll be okay. 'Bye." I took a few steps, then turned. "Thanks." If I got back into the asylum alive, then it would have been a wonderful night. I started off, and turned back again. I wanted to fix the lie I'd told. "Solly . . . Mr. Gruber—"

"Solly is good. Call me Solly."

I nodded. "Uh, Solly . . . My real name is Dave Caros, not Rubino. 'Bye." I turned and ran.

"Daveleh, about Irma Lee's party—"

I stopped. How could I have forgotten?

"Should I come to your HHB, or what?"

"No—I mean, I can meet you somewhere."

Solly said we should meet on this corner at eleven.

"All right." I started to run.

"Wait, boychik."

At this rate I was never going to get back.

"Here." Solly pulled a dollar out of his pocket. "Put it with the other one so it shouldn't be lonely."

I stood still, amazed. I stared at Solly. He looked like he needed the money more than I did. I swallowed hard. "Thanks!"

And then I really ran. I tripped over a branch and kept running. I made as much noise as a stampeding elephant. I sprang over the low wall and left the park. I bounded across Saint Nicholas Terrace and raced toward the HHB.

All the lights were still off, and the street was quiet. My knees felt weak from relief.

The branch of the tree I'd climbed before arched high above my head. I tried to climb the fence, but I couldn't get a grip on the iron posts.

The trolley rumbled by half a block away on Broadway. People who worked at the HHB might be getting off. They could arrive any second.

A light winked on in the basement of the asylum.

I was going to get caught.

I backed across the street and into an alley, crashing

into an empty ash can. The sound thundered in the silent street. I held my breath. No more lights came on in the HHB.

What about the can? I could stand on it and get a boost up the fence. As quietly as possible, I carried it across the street to the fence and climbed up on it. It started to buckle, then held my weight. But the crossbar was still too high to reach. I lugged the can back to the alley and stood there, thinking.

It was hopeless. I wasn't going to get in till they opened the front gate. I'd go in side by side with Mr. Doom. He'd do to me what he'd done to Leon. Or worse.

A horse and cart clattered down the street and stopped at the side entrance. I hid behind the ash can. It was the milk delivery for the orphanage.

The milkman climbed down from his perch behind the horse. He went to the back of the cart and lifted out two small wagons. Then he moved to the other side of the cart where I couldn't see him.

A man, wearing pajamas like mine, came out of the side door of the asylum. He was the man I'd seen in the basement, the janitor. As he came down the path, I heard him humming. The last time he'd been singing.

He stopped humming and said, "I swear you come earlier every day, Pat." I heard the lock turn and the gate swing open. He disappeared behind the cart where the milkman was.

"Hello, Ed. It's high time you were up and looking after the little brats."

"I'm the janitor. I don't look after anybody."

Could I sneak by them?

If I couldn't see them because the cart was in the way, they couldn't see me. It was my only chance. I darted across the street and crouched on my side of the cart. The horse shuffled a step and shook its head. This was it. The horse had given me away.

No, it was ordinary horse behavior. The milkman didn't come around to investigate.

"Did your cousin get a radio?"

"He did." The milkman laughed. "At least a hundred people packed into his room to hear the thing wheeze and crackle . . . Careful, there . . . That's it, then."

The milkman was going to drive away, leaving me staring at Ed!

"Let's go."

I watched their feet from under the cart. They wheeled the milk down the path to the asylum, leaving the gate open behind them. They disappeared into the basement entrance. I ran through the gate and started for the front door. Then I stopped. The milkman could come out any second and see me. I rushed back to hide in the bushes that lined the fence. At least I was inside.

I waited. A light came on in a window on the fourth floor. Any second they'd ring a wake-up bell.

Finally the milkman came out. A minute later he was clopping down the street and I was dashing toward the front door.

I prayed for it to still be open. I pounded up the steps. My hand stopped an inch from the doorknob. Mr. Doom could be in there, waiting.

I turned the doorknob. The door was open. Mazel tov, like the parrot said. Congratulations. I inched the door open. The lobby was dark. I stepped inside.

Somebody grabbed my arm and slammed the door. "Gotcha!"

CHAPTER
14

"STINKING KID—COULD have gotten me fired. If I hadn't seen you through the window . . ."

It was Mr. Meltzer. He pulled me to the stairs, squeezing my arm so tight my fingers tingled. At least it wasn't Mr. Doom. Mike said Mr. Meltzer didn't hit.

"Bloom will kill you," he growled. "Serves you right. I'd like to kill you myself."

He was taking me to Mr. Doom! "I didn't do anything. I just took a walk." My heart banged around crazily.

He pulled me up the stairs and half-dragged me to the elevens' room. So he wasn't taking me to Mr. Doom after all. Thank you, Mr. Meltzer. Outside the door he stopped. "What's this?" He tugged on Solly's tie.

I'd forgotten all about it. "It's my grandfather's."

Mr. Meltzer untied it and stuffed it into his pocket.

He opened the door to the room, which was dim in the almost-dawn. Everybody was still asleep. One of Mike's legs stuck out past the edge of the bed. It shook.

The bell clanged. They all sat up and started to make their beds. Nobody rolled over to get another minute of sleep. They were too well behaved. Or too scared.

"Get moving, all of you. Hurry up," Mr. Meltzer yelled. "Make your beds and line up for showers." He turned to me. "I'll take you to Mr. Bloom after breakfast."

He *was* taking me! My heart started banging again.

Everybody heard. Kids moved out of my way as I walked to my bed. I felt how comfortably my legs moved, how my arms swung at my side. After Mr. Doom was through with me, would someone have to carry me?

I followed everybody to the showers. Kids ahead of me stumbled because they were staring at me instead of looking where they were going.

"Stop looking at me!" I was going to be fine. What I'd done wasn't so bad. I had come back, hadn't I?

"What did you do?" Mike bounced up and down next to me.

"I snuck out."

"It's been nice knowing you."

Mr. Meltzer stood over me during breakfast. That meant Moe couldn't eat my food, even though he was next to me as usual. But it was a waste, because I wasn't hungry.

The bell rang. Breakfast was over.

Mr. Meltzer put his hand on my shoulder. "You stay."

"Here, kid," Moe said. "My lucky penny. It'll protect you."

I took it. It couldn't hurt.

"But don't spend it," he added. "I want it back."

"Dave," Mike said. "You need your strength." He handed me something and slapped my arm. "Good luck."

He'd given me half a roll. I ate it while everybody filed out of the basement. I could tell Mr. Doom I'd gone home last night because my brother was sick. Or I'd pretend I was a sleepwalker, and as soon as I realized I was outside the Home, I hurried back—because I knew it was against the rules, and I hated kids who broke rules. If he didn't believe me, I'd get away from him. He was big. He'd be slow. I'd outrun him.

"Let's go," Mr. Meltzer said.

I didn't move.

He yanked me up by my jacket. "Come on." He pulled me toward the stairs.

I made myself as heavy as I could. On the stairs, I latched on to the banister, even though I knew it was cowardly.

Mr. Meltzer pried my hand loose. "Don't make me carry you."

I didn't want him to carry me in to Mr. Doom. I stopped fighting him.

He knocked on the door of Mr. Doom's office. Then he held me by the elbow, and we stepped inside.

"The new boy, Dave Caros. I caught him trying to run away."

That was a lie! He caught me coming back.

"Sit down, son," Mr. Doom rumbled.

I sat. Mr. Meltzer left and closed the door behind him.

"I wasn't running away. I was just—"

Mr. Doom's face reddened. "Did I ask you a question?"

"No, but . . ."

He reached for his yardstick.

"Sir. No, sir."

His voice went back to a rumble. "I think we should have a chat. Don't you agree?"

"Yes, sir. I agree, sir."

He leaned back in his seat. "Mrs. Bloom and I love the finer things in life, the theater, concerts." He rumbled a chuckle. "Mrs. Bloom's little hobby is following the doings of high society."

What was he talking about? But keep yapping, and stay away from that yardstick.

"So one might wonder at my choice of vocation. I admit it's a sacrifice, but someone has to do the dirty work. Someone has to take in children like you." He straightened his spectacles. "Otherwise, you'd have nowhere to go. However, it's like putting a rattlesnake to your bosom."

Bosom! I didn't even want to laugh.

"Snakes bite, and chances are you'll be bitten. What else can you expect from paupers and orphans?" He shook his huge head sadly. "But in a civilized society . . ."

This was like a Mr. Cluck lecture about how hard we were to teach. I settled back in the leather chair. I was still scared, but I could see I wasn't in danger this second.

He droned on about how much he'd improved the HHB. I looked around the office again. We should have electric fires in our rooms. I looked at the knickknack case.

"You're a typical orphan. I see . . ."

My eyes snapped to Mr. Doom and then back to the knickknacks. Papa's carving was there! On the second shelf, next to a china donkey.

"Your father was an indigent, a bum. Your step-mother—"

"At least my papa wasn't a thief," I blurted out.

Mr. Doom's face got so red it glowed. He reached for the yardstick. His spectacles slipped sideways. He looked crazy. I should have run. But instead, I went for the carving.

I didn't reach it. The flat side of the yardstick smashed into my shoulder and threw me against his desk.

"Thief!" he yelled. "You call me . . ."

He hit me again. The edge of the stick tore across my neck and the end cut into my cheek and ear. Drops of blood fell onto the carpet.

I think I screamed. I ran to put the desk between us. He came after me.

"*Your* papa!" he hollered. "You compare . . ." The yardstick caught me in the chest. I staggered back. My head hit the corner of the desk.

For a second everything went black. When I opened my eyes, he was standing over me with the yardstick raised over his head. And I realized—he didn't care what he did to me.

CHAPTER
15

I SCRAMBLED AWAY. The blow got me on my calf.
Mr. Doom raised the yardstick. I twisted. The
stick broke on the desk. He threw his half aside—
clenched his fist—came after me.

"I'll show you . . ."

One punch—I'd be dead. *He wouldn't care.* He was
blocking the door. I couldn't get out.

"Help!" I screamed. "Papa!"

No help—no Papa. He swung. I ducked. His fist
grazed my forehead. My ears rang.

Soon he'd catch me. Nobody would save me.

He swung. I ducked. Missed. Reached for me with
his other hand. Missed. I had to get away. Couldn't.
Maybe . . .

Climbed onto his desk. Might get around him.

He bellowed. "Filthy feet . . ." Lunged at me.

Nowhere to go. Back, I'd fall. Stumbled forward.

He lurched—clutched at me—pulled me in. He had me!

Face—inches away—red—mouth open—sweaty skin—crooked glasses.

Grabbed them! Grabbed his specs—held them tight.

"What—where—" One arm let me go. Roar. "My spec—" Roar. "Give me—" Other arm had me.

I squirmed—yanked—twisted—got free! Got free!

"Where—" Roar. "You'd better—" Roar.

Crossed the desktop. Jumped off. Papa's carving—knickknack cabinet—rushed at it.

"Come—" Roar. "Wait till—" Swung his arms—trying to find me.

Cabinet locked! I pulled at it. Things rattled. Locked.

Feeling his way around the desk—opening a drawer. Extra glasses!

Run! Go! I dropped his spectacles and ran.

Mr. Meltzer—outside the door. "Come on." He took my arm. I pulled away—shut the office door. He took my arm again.

Inside—did he find his glasses? Was he coming?

Mr. Meltzer led me to a staircase. I kept looking back. Was he coming?

On the stairs I made it up three steps and then stopped. I couldn't go any farther. Mr. Meltzer waited. I should keep going. The stairwell door could open, and Mr. Doom could be there.

"I didn't . . ." Mr. Meltzer's voice was softer than

usual, less bark in it. He was frowning. He always frowned. He coughed. "You shouldn't have run away." Same old voice.

I didn't run away. I came back, didn't I?

But I would escape. I'd sworn it. I would escape.

My knee trembled even though he hadn't hit me there. I couldn't make it stop.

"Ready?"

I looked up at the next landing. I took a step, then another, then another. We went to the infirmary. When she saw me, the nurse said, "Bloom?"

Mr. Meltzer said, "He tried to run away."

"Smart kid."

Mr. Meltzer didn't answer. He left, and the nurse said Mr. Doom wouldn't come after me there.

"If I didn't need this job," she said, dabbing at my cheek with a soapy washcloth, "I'd . . ."

She didn't finish the sentence. The soap stung. But the ice she put on my forehead felt good. When she cleaned off the cut on my leg, she said she had to call a doctor.

While she gave the doctor's telephone number to the operator, I started to cry. Not because of Mr. Doom. Because the nurse was so nice. Pretty stupid to cry because somebody was nice.

The cut on my neck wasn't so bad, and the nurse was able to bandage it up herself. My ear and cheek didn't even need bandages. The bump on my forehead throbbed, but it wasn't bleeding, so it only got ice.

When the doctor came, he sewed up the cut on my leg—four stitches. He asked where the other boy was, the one I'd fought. The nurse said she didn't know. For a second, I thought about telling him who beat me up. But if I did, and Mr. Doom found out, he'd finish killing me. The doctor said it was terrible how the older boys picked on the younger ones.

After the doctor left, the nurse made me stay in the infirmary. That was good—I was safe there. Sometimes I dozed, sometimes I watched her. Sometimes I touched my forehead or one of the bandages, and she'd tell me to leave them alone. But mostly I kept my eyes closed and went over the fight—especially the moment when I knew Mr. Doom didn't care what he did to me. I went over and over the moments before he hit me, when I knew he would. Flinching, trying to get away, not knowing how bad it would be.

Nobody had rescued me. I'd rescued myself. I remembered taking his glasses—the sweat on his forehead, the glossy, slick feel of his nose. I thought of what Gideon had said when he left for Chicago, that I'd be all right. And I was. If Gideon had been in that office instead of me, he'd be dead.

But Gideon wouldn't have been there. He wouldn't have had the guts to sneak out of the asylum in the first place. He would have let Mr. Doom get away with stealing Papa's carving.

Don't think about Gideon or Papa. Think about

how to rescue yourself. How to rescue the carving and then yourself.

Mr. Doom kept his office locked when he wasn't there. Plus the cabinet was locked. Breaking the glass in the cabinet door wouldn't do any good. The panes were too small, separated by wooden latticing that the carving wouldn't fit through. I needed the key.

If I had dynamite, I'd sneak downstairs late at night and light it. The door to his office would blow in, and I'd step inside. I'd open the top drawer of his desk. The key to the cabinet would be there. I'd snatch the carving just as a gang of prefects thundered downstairs. I'd race outside and run to the oak tree and climb over. Then I'd run and never look back.

I'd find Irma Lee, and she'd be so glad to see me.

By suppertime I was hungry, even though I ached all over and the bump on my head never stopped throbbing. I ate with the nurse. The food was better than the glop they served in the basement, and she didn't eat any of my portion. After supper, she told me I could leave. It was six-thirty. I didn't want to go, but I couldn't hide out in the nurse's office forever.

I wondered if Mr. Doom was looking for me.

I didn't see him. Everyone I passed stared at my bandages and the bump. The elevens were in the auditorium, but I didn't want to go there. I wanted to sleep.

Our room was empty. When I put on my pajamas I had to be careful not to rip the bandages off. In bed,

I fell asleep instantly. I didn't hear the bell ring for the end of study hall or the end of recess, and I didn't hear the elevens come in, and I didn't hear the bell ring for lights-out.

The first thing I heard was someone whispering, "Dave, buddy!" in my ear. Whoever it was also shook my aching shoulder.

"Watch it!" I sat up, feeling stiff.

"Shh."

All the elevens were crowded around my bed.

"We want to know what happened, buddy." Mike bobbed up and down.

"Tell us what Mr. Doom did to you," somebody said. In the dark, I couldn't tell who. Then he coughed. Alfie.

"And why Mr. Meltzer took you to him," someone else said.

"He went out last night," Mike said.

"So what, buddy?" The whisper was raspy. It must be that know-it-all, Harvey. "We go out."

"He went *out* out. Outside."

Why were they asking me when Mike had all the answers?

"Outside the fence?" somebody asked.

Mike snapped his fingers and cracked his knuckles. "Naturally outside the fence."

"You know the oak tree near the fence?" I reached down to make sure the bandage was still in place on my leg. It was.

A few heads nodded. Somebody said, "Yeah."

"You know how one of the branches reaches over the fence?"

No one said anything.

"There's a crack in the trunk this high up . . ." I explained how I got out.

Mike said, "See? I told you."

"Where did you go?" one of the twins asked.

"Did you go into Saint Nicholas Park?" the other one said.

"He wouldn't," the first twin said.

"The park by Saint Nicholas Terrace? Sure I did. Why not?"

"They found a dead body in there last year." Mike sat on his bed and bounced.

"I saw something white on the ground," I said, hamming it up. "It could have been a bone."

"I think there's poison ivy in there, buddy," Alfie said. He coughed. Nobody said anything till he stopped.

"There were fang marks on the body," Eli said. "They say the murderer was an enormous wolf."

"I heard breathing," I said, "but I thought it was the wind. And I saw these yellow eyes—"

Alfie started coughing again, and this time he didn't stop. Everybody ran back to bed. The door opened.

"Alfie? You need the nurse?"

He went on coughing, and Mr. Meltzer said he was taking him to the nurse. Then he yelled, "When I get back, everybody better be asleep, or else!" He stopped at my bed. "Here. I saved this for you." He dropped Solly's tie on my pillow and left. I heard Alfie coughing all the way down the hall.

I pulled my suitcase out from under the bed and put the tie inside, where the carving should have been. So now I had my fake grandpa's tie, but Mr. Doom had the only thing left of my real papa.

CHAPTER 16

I GOT BACK in bed and closed my eyes.

"Why did you run away, buddy?" Mike asked.

They were all around me again.

"I didn't run away," I said, sitting up. "He beat me up for running away, but I came back." The cut on my neck hurt. "Anyway, do *you* like it here?"

"Why did you come back?" Eli asked.

Before I could answer, Harvey said, "He didn't have any place to go. Who would take him in? He's a whole orphan."

"Three-quarters!" I said.

"There's no such—"

"He wouldn't need anybody," Mike said, stopping the argument. "He can take care of himself."

"Let him answer, buddy," Eli said.

"He doesn't—" Harvey started.

111

"Shh," at least five boys said.

"Why does everybody call each other buddy?" I asked.

Lots of kids whispered at the same time, "We're buddies, not bullies."

"We eat together," Mike said, "sleep together, do everything together. But we're not brothers, so we're buddies."

Eli said, "We look out for each other."

Gideon should hear about this. He might learn something. Then again, he was just a brother.

"Even if I'm a half and you're only a whole," Harvey said, "I'll look out for you."

"So tell us why you came back," Mike said.

"Because of my papa's carving, buddy." I told them about it, and I told them where it was.

Somebody whistled. Somebody else said, "Oy vay!"

"You can kiss your carving good-bye, buddy," Harvey said. "You'll never get it back."

"Yes I will, buddy." He thought he knew everything. But he didn't know me.

"How?" Mike asked eagerly.

I didn't know yet, but I would.

"He won't get it," Harvey said, "because it's impossible."

"We'll all work on it," Eli said. "What did you do after you came out of the park?"

"First I saw a Pierce-Arrow—"

The lights came on. I froze. Mr. Doom had come to get me.

Everybody scattered.

It was Mr. Meltzer. "I told you to go to sleep. I'm sitting right outside the door. If I hear so much as loud breathing, you get no meals tomorrow."

"How's Alfie?" Eli asked.

"Just go to sleep." Mr. Meltzer turned out the lights and slammed the door.

This time everybody stayed in bed. Even though I'd been up most of last night, I couldn't fall asleep. The bump throbbed, and I felt like the milkman's horse and cart had ridden over me.

I rolled onto my stomach to get more comfortable, but that was worse. I rolled back.

Solly might take me when I ran away for good. I could help him. I could feed Bandit. I could groan when he needed a groaner. I'd ask him when we met for Irma Lee's party.

But how could I go to the party? I wouldn't be able to get out. Mr. Meltzer would be watching me like a hawk.

In the middle of the night I woke up from a dream. I'd dreamed I was in a room with a coffin. I went up to it and saw that Papa was inside. He sat up. I said, "You're alive!" But he said, "No, I'm dead." And I thought, this isn't so bad if I can still talk to him when he's dead.

Then I woke up. My blanket had fallen off, and I was freezing, except for the bump on my head, which felt hot. I had to go to the toilet. Mr. Meltzer was right outside the door, wide awake. He escorted me to the toilet and waited till I was done.

I woke up once more before morning. Mr. Meltzer was standing over me. I sat up, scared.

"Go back to sleep," he said. "I was just making sure you hadn't gone anywhere."

Alfie was waiting for us at our table when we got to breakfast. Before the bullies came, he showed us the bag of rock candy the nurse had given him. He said he'd share it at recess. And then he sat on the bag, so the bullies wouldn't see it.

When Moe arrived and saw my bandages, he didn't want his penny back. "It's unlucky. Good thing I loaned it to you or I might have depended on it."

"See, Moe," Eli said from across the table, "good deeds pay off. If you left our food alone, you might get even luckier."

"Nah. I don't think so."

I left the basement surrounded by my buddies. On the stairs Mike was bobbing next to me, and Eli was right behind me. Eli said, "So what happened after you went through the park?"

"I saw—"

"Uh-oh," Eli said softly.

I looked up. Mr. Doom stood on the landing above us. I turned to run back downstairs.

Mike caught my arm. "Don't run," he whispered.

"Don't run," Eli whispered.

"Good morning, boys," Mr. Doom boomed.

"Good morning, sir," everybody said. Everybody but me. I moved my lips, but nothing came out.

"Having fun with your pals, boys?"

"Yes, sir."

He saw me and started down the steps. Boys flattened themselves against the stairway walls to let him by. There were a million boys behind me. I couldn't run. He came closer, step by step. I fought to keep my breakfast down.

"What's this, son?" He touched the bandage on my neck.

I jumped down a step. Didn't he know he gave it to me? Eli and Mike were mouthing words at me. I couldn't tell what they were saying.

Mr. Doom's face started getting red. "Don't you know how to answer—"

"A cut, sir. Just a cut, sir." My voice was a squeak.

"That's better. I hope you got it from playing, not from fighting."

"From playing, sir."

"Be more careful next time. I can't have my boys hurting themselves. Now get going, or you'll miss your studies."

I stumbled up the stairs. Didn't he recognize me? Was he that blind even with his glasses on? Had he beaten up so many boys that we all looked alike to him? Or was he completely nuts?

CHAPTER 17

When we got to our classroom, a man and a woman were in the front of the room, and Mr. Cluck wasn't there at all. The woman wore trousers. I'd never seen a woman in pants before.

"Who are they?" I asked Mike.

"He's Mr. Hillinger, the art teacher. He's nice, but he's crazy. I don't know who she is."

I hoped he was better than the art teacher who came around to our class at P.S. 42, who taught us over and over about the color wheel and showed us pictures of what famous artists painted three hundred years ago.

"Boys," Mr. Hillinger said, "you may remember today for . . . high point of your child—of your life possibly." He talked so fast I wondered how he breathed. And he never finished what he was saying. He rushed around the room, handing out fat black crayons and big sheets of paper, which he put on the floor next to our desks. "Today . . . draw from a model . . . Heady experience . . . Draw on the floor, because your desks aren't big enough. Our model is the pretty young . . . in the unusual . . . She's Miss Hillinger, my sister."

Miss Hillinger wasn't pretty and she wasn't young. She had straight gray hair, a long face, and baggy cheeks. She looked a lot like Mr. Hillinger.

". . . Wearing my best trousers, so you can see what her legs are doing when she poses."

Mike started drawing violins in his notebook with his crayon. The twins were whispering. Harvey tapped a rhythm on the top of his desk. Eli read a book hidden in his lap. I watched Mr. Hillinger.

After he finished giving out the paper, he dug into a brown paper bag and pulled out a newspaper, which he waved at us. "Mine accident in Michigan . . . Jailbreak attempt here in . . . Houdini mourners . . . Better use for this." He covered Mr. Cluck's desk with newspaper. Then he put more newspaper across Mr. Cluck's chair.

"Allow me, dear." He helped Miss Hillinger step onto Mr. Cluck's chair and from there onto Mr. Cluck's desk.

Standing on a teacher's desk had to be against every one of the six thousand and twelve rules of the HHB. Mike stopped drawing. The twins stopped whispering. A few kids giggled.

"Now, Miss Hillinger will take . . . and you will draw her. Draw her big. Don't worry . . . Plenty of paper . . . First pose is three minutes—hurry! On the floor, all of you. Don't bother with fingers or Miss . . . her nose or her . . . hairstyle."

We made a lot of noise getting on the floor. My right heel knocked into the bandage on my leg. It *hurt*.

"Ready, my . . ." Mr. Hillinger said, while pulling his watch out of his pocket.

"Ready, Siegfried." Miss Hillinger put her hands on her hips and twisted to her left, turning her head so she was looking away from us at the blackboard behind her.

I stared. How could I do a drawing in three minutes?

"Go!" Mr. Hillinger said. "See how she's turned? Show the twist . . . This is gesture drawing you're . . . It has a long and respectable . . ."

I thought of the twist in a pretzel, and I drew a spiral in the middle of the page. Then I looked at Miss Hillinger again. The folds in her blouse sort of followed the spiral I had drawn. I kind of sketched them around it. How much time had gone by? Her feet were apart, and she was leaning on the toe of her right foot. I drew in her legs. Something was wrong. It looked like she was kicking with her right foot.

" . . . examples by Leonardo and Rem . . . And even Grosz or Picass— Stop. Time's up . . . Now let me see . . ."

Miss Hillinger relaxed. Kids were laughing. I didn't stop. I couldn't. She didn't have a head. I put in a circle, which looked all wrong. Then I stopped, since I couldn't remember exactly how she'd been standing. She didn't have any arms in my drawing, and she had a circle for a head, and she only took up a quarter of the page. I wished he'd given us more time.

Mr. Hillinger threaded his way between the desks, stepping over our drawings. "Fine, Alfie. Harvey, interesting. I tell everyone they should see what my orphans . . . Nice and big, Eli. Mike, my sister is not a violin, although . . . Ah." He stopped at my desk. ". . . You caught some of the gesture. Very good. What's your name?" I saw him notice the bump on my head and my bandages.

"Dave Caros."

"Excellent, Dave. You have the beginnings of an eye. Now, Ira, let me see . . ."

He said something about lots of drawings, but he didn't say anybody else had an eye or the beginnings of one.

At the front of the room again, he said, "Gesture drawings. You showed the . . . what the model—Miss Hillinger—was doing. Here. Look. Perhaps I can . . ."

In front of me, Ira was trying to draw on Danny's arm. Danny was pulling away and both of them were giggling.

"How often does he come?" I asked Mike.

"Mondays and Fridays."

Mr. Hillinger tacked a sheet of paper to Mr. Cluck's corkboard. "Two minutes, Louise." He handed his watch to one of the twins. "Fred, when I say 'go,' start.

Then say 'stop' when two min . . . Ready, Louise? Give me a hard one. It won't matter if I—"

"All right, Siggy."

Some kids snickered at the nickname, Siggy.

"Marvelous model, my . . . She has . . ."

Miss Hillinger put one hand on her hip and bent over. With the other hand she seemed to be reaching for something on the desktop—under her feet. The pose made her look like an old lady with a backache, picking something up from the floor.

"Go." Mr. Hillinger stared at her for a moment. Then, with a single line, he drew the curve of her back and her rear end and the back edge of her trousers.

It just took him a few seconds—whoosh, and there it was. Everybody stopped talking.

"It helps if . . . anatomy, but you . . . Someday I'll teach . . ." He used the side of the crayon to shade in the arm she'd put on her hip, which was sticking up in the air. He kept talking while he worked, but now he was talking to himself. "More shading . . . mass of hair . . . Can't see her face . . . Now the arm—use a line . . . Vary pressure, make it interesting . . . Negative space . . ." He stopped drawing Miss Hillinger, even though she wasn't all drawn in, and drew in the top of the desk and part of the blackboard. When he got to the edge of the page, he kept going, drawing out onto Mr. Cluck's corkboard. He went out a few inches and then went back to the paper. "No fingers, as I told . . . other arm goes . . . Nice pose . . ."

When Fred said, "Stop," Mr. Hillinger was drawing in the side of the desk.

It was like magic. I was grinning, and I wanted to clap. I looked around. Lots of kids were smiling. Eli was. Fred and Jeff were. Mike was drawing violins.

"This is the gesture. Feel her trying to reach . . . And weight, she has weight. Now you . . . Turn over your paper. And remember, big. Fill your page. We want . . ."

Miss Hillinger stretched, with her arms going straight up—and she stayed that way.

I tried to think about everything he'd told us: to make her big, to get the gesture, not to worry about fingers or noses. If she was going to be big, her waist should land in the middle of the page. I started there. Her chest swelled up from her stretching. I made it round, and I used the length of my crayon to do her arms, two fat lines going straight up, and two short lines going sideways for her hands. I did her legs the same way.

"You may stop, dear," Mr. Hillinger said.

"You made her legs too short, Dave," Harvey said from behind me. "She looks like a dwarf."

"He made her big, like we were supposed to," Mike said.

I looked at Harvey's drawing. In it, Miss Hillinger wasn't any bigger than my fist. I looked back at mine. It was terrible, but you could tell she was stretching. I had gotten the gesture, sort of.

Mr. Hillinger didn't come around this time. "Now

you will . . . You're going to draw Miss Hill . . . by not drawing her."

Huh?

"You're going to . . . the space around her, and the hole that's left will be Miss . . . Here. Watch. I'll show you what . . ." He went back to his drawing, which was still tacked to the corkboard. "You may . . . I forgot to draw in the front of my sister's trousers . . ."—he drew in a line for the edge of the desk behind Miss Hillinger—". . . and the back of her arm. You'll notice what . . ." With the side of the crayon he shaded in the wall behind the desk and then drew another line, for the bottom of the blackboard. Then he shaded the blackboard darker than the wall. But he didn't shade the space where Miss Hillinger's legs and arms belonged— and they popped out, white, but solid because of the space he left for them. I didn't know you could do that.

"You need different . . . use anything, but charcoal is . . . Charcoal and erasers." He walked around the room, handing out the supplies, and giving us a fresh sheet of paper.

The charcoal came in sticks, thinner than a pencil and lighter than a leaf. I tested it on my paper. It drew like silk, and the line was blacker than the crayon.

". . . Fifteen-minute pose, so take something you can hold, Louise." Mr. Hillinger looked around the room. "There. Would you like that? You can . . ." He pointed at a low stool in the front corner near the door. She nodded.

"There. That's . . ." He lifted the stool to the top of the desk. Miss Hillinger put her right foot on it. Then she rested her right hand on the leg that leaned on the stool, and put her left hand on the back of her neck.

"Beautiful pose . . . Look at . . . Beautiful. But can you . . . Start now, boys. Fifteen minutes will pass . . ."

Behind her, the top of the blackboard ended above her ears, and the bottom ended a little above the knee of the leg she was standing on. I drew a horizontal line near the top of the page, leaving a space for her head. Two-thirds of the way down the page I drew another line for the bottom of the blackboard. This time I left a wide space for the distance from one leg to the other.

I started shading in the blackboard. It would have been easy to shade in the part that was nowhere near her, where I couldn't make a mistake. But I wanted to do what Mr. Hillinger had shown us. I wanted to see if I could make her pop out of the page, the way he had.

Her head was down. I wanted to get the way it drooped. I shaded the blackboard by the back of her head, trying to get the curve from her shoulder, up through the back of her neck, around the mound of her hand to the top of her head. I shaded through her wrist. Dumb. I had sliced off one of her arms. I erased the place where the wrist should have been. It was fun, like drawing backwards, making the black disappear.

"No outlining . . . Only what's around her. An artist has . . ." Mr. Hillinger walked between our desks, giving advice. "Don't just draw in one place . . . spot to spot. It'll all come together. Nice start, Bernie. Keep your arms moving, get your bodies . . ."

I moved to Miss Hillinger's right arm, the one leaning on her leg. The elbow pointed away from me. I wouldn't have known how to outline the arm, since it looked much shorter than it actually was. Luckily, I only had to shade around it. I tried to get the diamond space between her arm and her leg and chest exactly right. I got it.

"Use your erasers. You should compose the whole . . ."

Her head was too far to the left. If I kept going, it wouldn't meet her shoulders. The head was the best part of the drawing. I didn't want to erase it, but it would take too long to move everything else. I could copy the head where it belonged, then erase the old head. But that would mean outlining, cheating. How much time was left, anyway?

I looked to see where Mr. Hillinger was. Right behind me, watching me, seeing the stupid head miles away from the stupid body.

CHAPTER 18

I WANTED TO cover the drawing, but he'd already seen it. So I just got back to work. I erased the shaded blackboard where Miss Hillinger's head should really be. That way I could look at the old head that I liked while putting in the new one.

"Courage, Dave." Mr. Hillinger touched my shoulder and then went on down the aisle. I didn't know what he meant. I didn't need courage here, in the classroom. Then I forgot about it, looking at Miss Hillinger and working on the head. The new one wasn't as good as the old one, but at least it was in the right place. I didn't erase the old head, because I liked it, and started working on her shoulder and left arm.

"You gave her two heads, buddy. Boy, are you lousy at art."

I turned to see Harvey's drawing. His paper was almost all shaded. In the middle was a tiny figure, leaning on one leg.

"My two heads are in my drawing, buddy," I said. "Too bad your two heads—"

"Time's up. Stop, everybody."

My leg ached and itched under the bandage. I looked at what I'd done. Miss Hillinger had two heads and disconnected parts of the rest of her. It looked like she had been chopped in pieces. Even so, the places I *had* done did jump out at you, and the foot leaning on the stool had weight like it was supposed to. You could feel it, pushing down.

Mr. Hillinger walked through the aisles again, inspecting. "This is fine . . . Louise, look . . . I never stop being . . ."

She climbed down from the desk and walked around the edge of the room. I hoped she wouldn't come near me and see herself with two heads.

Mr. Hillinger took Bernie's drawing and Eli's and Harvey's and mine. He tacked the four drawings to the corkboard, where they all looked rotten next to his. Eli's drawing was big, so big that half of Miss Hillinger's head and her left leg below the knee were off the page. Bernie's drawing was the best. Miss Hillinger wasn't as big as she was in mine, but she didn't have two heads, and the pose was right. I wondered if Mr. Hillinger had picked Eli's, Harvey's, and mine to show how much we had to learn.

"What do I always say?" Mr. Hillinger asked, standing next to our drawings.

"You can't do a bad drawing till you're a grown-up," Mike whispered.

"You can't do a bad drawing till you're a grown-up," Mr. Hillinger said. He pointed to Bernie's drawing. "What I like best . . . See how Bernie changed the depth in the shadow around . . . See how dark it is here." He pointed. "And what a soft gray . . . Very good, Bernie."

I wondered why he didn't say anything about how well Bernie had drawn Miss Hillinger, how she had the right number of arms and legs and heads, all more or less in the right place.

"And Harvey's is wonderful too, boys."

I didn't have to look at Harvey. I could feel him swelling up.

"It's small, and I told . . . work big, but Harvey is . . . He draws with the directness . . . more like a six-year-old than an eleven . . . Hold on to that, Harvey."

I turned around, grinning. Harvey didn't think it was wonderful to draw like a six-year-old. His face was bright red.

"These two . . ." Mr. Hillinger touched my drawing and Eli's.

I got ready. My hands clenched, and I felt my face get red too. He was going to tell everybody how bad mine was.

". . . Have excellent compositions. Your eye

moves . . ." He swung his arm in a circle over our drawings. "See? Yes, Harvey?"

Excellent composition. Excellent. I wished I knew what he meant about your eye moving in a circle.

"But Dave's has two heads and the body is in pieces, and Eli's is missing part of the head and part of the leg."

"Two heads are fine. Not on . . . but in a drawing . . . you're searching, and sometimes two heads—"

"Siggy, excuse me. It's five after ten. You said to tell you when it was—"

Mr. Hillinger dashed to the front of the room. "Go, Louise. Meet me . . . Hurry. Don't tell . . ." She was out the door. "He'll be here any . . ." He lifted the stool off the desk.

Who was coming? Mr. Doom? My bump started throbbing.

Mr. Hillinger whipped the newspaper off the desk and off Mr. Cluck's chair. "Boys, back in your . . . Up off the floor. Put your drawings on your desks." He handed our drawings back to us and started folding newspapers wildly. "At my other schools I don't have . . . Sorry, boys. You did fine . . . I—"

Mr. Cluck opened the door.

"Good morning, Mr. Cl—Gluck. As usual your boys were excel . . . I don't know how you . . . See you next week, boys. Save your drawings for when you're famous." He left.

Now the HHB had two things I liked: the elevens being buddies and Mr. Hillinger's art lessons.

For the rest of the morning I ignored Mr. Cluck's lesson about what was wrong with us. First I drew Alfie, who sat on my right. I did it as a gesture drawing, working on showing the way he hunched his shoulders. Then I tried to draw Mike, but it was like trying to draw a live butterfly. So then I drew Mr. Cluck, with his mouth open—his gesture.

After that I turned to a clean page in my notebook.

Dear Papa,

I guess you know where I am and who put me here and who didn't come here with me.

My eyes started to prick. I didn't want to cry.

So I won't write about that. I just want to tell you about the art teacher here. You were an artist, so I think you'll be interested. Did you ever hear of gesture drawings? Did you ever do one?

I described Mr. Hillinger and what he'd taught us and what I'd thought while I was drawing. At the end I wrote,

And Papa, I have the beginnings of an eye! I'm going to draw as much as I can, and someday maybe I'll be so good that I have a whole entire eye! Two maybe!

Then I wrote, "I miss you." And I signed it, "Your son, Dave the rascal. Dave the gesture artist."

In the next couple of weeks, while I thought about how to get the carving back and leave the HHB, I drew as often as I could. I had always liked to draw, but Papa had been the artist, not me. Now, though, I thought that I might be an artist too and keep art in the family. I figured Papa would like that.

The next week Mr. Hillinger had us do what he called line drawings of a vase filled with flowers. Line drawings were the opposite of shading. They were a new kind of outlining—I never heard anyone talk about the "sensitivity" of a line before.

One time Mr. Hillinger brought in magazine photographs for us to copy. Another day he gave out crayons, but he only let us use certain color combinations. Every class we did something new, and after every lesson I saw things a little differently.

Two weeks after the rent party, the doctor came and removed my stitches. He said I'd have the scar for a long while, maybe forever, which was good. I wanted a souvenir of the time I got the better of Mr. Doom.

As the days passed, I stopped waking up every morning wondering where I was. And I stopped expecting Mr. Doom to be hiding around every corner, waiting to jump out at me.

I got to like my buddies more and more. I'd had friends before I came, and once I had a brother, but I'd never had anything like this. For example, on Visiting Day (really half a day—Sunday afternoons) the visitors usually brought food. But not one single eleven ever ate his food then and there. They might take a taste to show appreciation, but they always set the rest aside for nighttime. After lights-out, Eli would divvy up the loot equally, no matter who had contributed and who hadn't.

Nobody visited me, but I got to eat as much as anybody else. And on Sunday night, December 5th, which was during Hanukkah, eating as much as anybody else meant eating *a lot*. The visitors brought at least twice as much as usual, and for the first time in the Home, I felt full, so full that I almost passed up a handful of dried dates and figs.

Another example of the buddies' loyalty was the time I drew on the photograph of Mr. Meltzer's family, which was on his table in the corner of our room. I pulled it out of its frame and drew mustaches and beards on the faces of his wife and his two daughters. I made each one different to go with the face. The goatee I put on Mrs. Meltzer was especially good. Papa would have laughed his head off.

Mr. Meltzer was so mad he slammed the picture down on his table and broke the glass. By then, I regretted doing it, because I was scared he'd drag me to Mr. Doom again. Mr. Meltzer yelled at us for ten minutes but nobody would tell who'd done it. In P.S. 42, somebody would have ratted inside of ten seconds.

I confessed. I couldn't let everybody be delivered to Mr. Doom because of me.

He didn't take me to Mr. Doom, but he made me skip breakfast and lunch and he didn't let me out at recess for a week. Plus I had to do stupid things over and over, like making my bed and shining my shoes and writing a thousand times, "I shall never deface a photograph again."

One more example of being buddies was the pillow fight one night after lights-out. We did it in absolute silence, and we kept it up for half an hour without the prefect outside the door hearing a thing. At the end one of the pillows exploded, and Reuben was covered with feathers. Eli tugged him to the window where it was a little brighter, and we spent a half hour holding in our giggles and plucking feathers one by one.

I even came to like Harvey, once I understood him. He was forever boasting about being a half and saying he was only here temporarily, till his mother came for him. And he kept bragging about her, how she was prettier than anybody else's mother, and smarter. But she didn't come to see him very often. In a month she only showed up once. When she didn't come, Harvey would hardly open his mouth for a few days afterwards.

And when she did come, she brought too much stuff. That may sound crazy when we were starved six days a week, but it was true. The time she came, she brought a honey cake, ten chocolate cupcakes, a whole salami, a thick woolen sweater, and a camera. See? It was too much.

But what really made me like Harvey was that he pretended the sweater was too small and gave it to Alfie.

Even though I liked my buddies and I liked Mr. Hillinger, the things I hated about the Hell Hole for Brats bothered me more and more as time went on.

I couldn't get used to the bells. Ting-a-ling—wake up. Ting-a-ling—go to sleep. Ting-a-ling—talk. Ting-a-ling—shut up.

I couldn't get used to being constantly cold. At home, the front room and the bedroom were cold in the winter, but the kitchen was always warm, especially in front of the coal stove. Gideon and I used to drag the couch cushions in there on freezing nights, and we'd sleep by the stove and be toasty warm.

Gideon! I couldn't get used to getting letters from him. One every week, saying how much he was learning, how kind Uncle Jack was, what a busybody the landlady was. He'd end every letter by telling me to write to him because he missed me. Too bad for him. I wasn't the one who got on a train to Chicago. I flushed every letter down the toilet.

Most of all—more than anything else—I couldn't get used to Papa being dead. I thought about him all the time. He'd be furious that Mr. Cluck never taught us anything. And Moe's food stealing—well, if he was alive, I'd never tell him about that. The food stealing was my problem.

He'd think Harvey was a windbag. But he'd like Mike and Eli, and he'd feel sorry for Alfie with his consumption. But Mr. Doom would make him as mad as he could get. He'd think that a man who would steal from an orphan was lower than a cockroach. He'd think a man who would endanger kids' health by keeping them cold and half starving them was even lower than that. He'd spit in Mr. Doom's face.

When I'd think like that, which was often, I'd get a huge lump in my throat that wouldn't go up and wouldn't go down. It would stay stuck, like I was stuck here, stuck being an orphan. A whole orphan. Harvey was right. Not three-quarters—I was a whole.

CHAPTER

19

$\mathcal{A}$S THE DATE came closer, I grew more and more frantic about getting out for Irma Lee's party. Mr. Meltzer had warned the other prefects to keep an eye on me when they were on hall duty. Most nights the prefect on duty would come to my bed to remind me not to try anything. My buddies said that would stop sooner or later. They said most of the prefects (although not Mr. Meltzer) liked to play poker when they were supposed to be watching us. They said the prefect in our hall would go back to the game eventually. But eventually never seemed to come.

The night before the party Mr. Meltzer was on duty again and I lay awake for a while trying to think of a plan. If I managed to get out, I had to be able to get back in too. I still didn't have the carving, and I wasn't going to leave for good until I did. I needed a ladder. Or a rope.

There might be rope in the supply closet in the basement. I fell asleep thinking about it. I don't know how long I slept, but Alfie's coughing woke me. It sounded like he was choking. I sat up, wondering if I should do something.

The door opened. Mr. Meltzer came in, and I lay back again, quick. He left with Alfie, and I closed my eyes, wishing Alfie would get better.

Then my eyes popped open. Mr. Meltzer had taken Alfie upstairs to the nurse. He wasn't guarding us. I could leave. I stood up. Nobody else seemed to be awake. I tucked my slippers in the waist of my pajamas. I was going on a rope hunt.

It didn't occur to me how dopey I was till I was creeping down the basement stairs. Mr. Meltzer wasn't going to stay upstairs forever. He would return to our room, and he would check my bed. I was done for.

I stood there, one foot up, one foot down. I didn't know if I should rush upstairs and hope I made it before Mr. Meltzer did. But if I went back, I wouldn't get the rope, and who knew when I'd have another chance?

The clock started bonging. I almost fell down the stairs. A lot of bongs—ten, eleven, or midnight.

It wasn't as dark in the basement as it had been on the stairs. There were small windows near the ceiling that let in a little light from the street outside. I could make out the shapes of the tables in the dining hall, and the huge pillars between the tables. Beyond them were the furnace and the coal chute, then Ed the janitor's room, then the laundry, and then, finally, miles from where I stood, the supply closet.

I edged through the dining hall. As soon as I stepped beyond the tables I stopped in surprise. There was no floor. It was just packed dirt. I hadn't noticed before, when I was wearing shoes. I didn't like it. Who knew what was crawling around in it. It was cold too, like everything else in the Heatless House of Bloom. And this was cold earth, like the ground in a graveyard.

Dirt was quieter than concrete, though.

I kept going. I passed the kitchen. The furnace. The coal chute.

The worst part would be going by Ed's room. I prayed for his door to be closed. Standing in the shadow of the furnace, I peeked out. It was open.

I inched forward, holding my breath, till I heard the most beautiful music—Ed was snoring. I walked a little faster.

Big sinks on my right, wringers on my left, clotheslines overhead. Mud squished between my toes—*ick!*—and there was a sucking noise whenever I took a step. I slowed down. There. That was quieter.

Mr. Meltzer had probably returned to our room by now. This minute he could be discovering I wasn't there. I kept on.

Now the ground felt drier. There was the supply

closet. I padded to it and turned the doorknob, slowly, slowly. It turned! It wasn't locked! I guess they didn't think anyone would raid it in the middle of the night with Ed only a few feet away.

I eased the door open. Don't squeak! Don't creak! As soon as the opening was wide enough, I slipped in.

It was too dark to see anything. Slowly, I stretched my arms out in front of me. Nothing. Air. I turned to my right and reached out. My hand touched something cold—metal—a bucket. I felt around next to it—something long, heavy—a crowbar.

It would take me weeks to find a rope in the dark, if there was a rope. I waved my arms gently over my head, taking tiny steps farther into the closet. And then I felt what I was hoping for, a light cord. I eased the door shut and pulled the cord.

The click sounded as loud as a cannon. I stopped breathing. I didn't hear anything from outside.

Shelves went all the way up to the ceiling. There was a ladder, a stepladder, a cardboard box full of tools on the lowest shelf, paint and paintbrushes on the shelf above, lightbulbs—lots of stuff. And at my feet, a big coil of rope. Thick rope, strong enough to hold my weight.

I heard something. *Slish. Slish.* Very soft. I reached for the light cord, missed it, got it, clicked out the light. *Slish slish.* Then the sucking noise. Someone was crossing the laundry.

I was trapped.

The sucking sound stopped and the slish slish started again. He was past the laundry. But why slish slish? Shoes wouldn't sound that way, but slippers might. Probably it was Ed, going to the toilet or prowling around because he'd heard a noise. My mind screamed at him, The toilet! The toilet! Go to the toilet!

He did. The slish slish passed the supply closet. A few minutes later, the toilet flushed, and I heard him again, coming close.

He stopped. Why?

> *"Sadie Lou was my first love.*
> *How I loved that Sadie Lou."*

He was singing!

There was an echo. It made his voice sound round and full.

The song said he met Sadie Lou when they were seven, and it was love at first sight. But she was rich and he was poor, so her parents sent her to a school far away.

> *"Annabelle was my next love.*
> *How I loved my Annabelle."*

War came, and Annabelle wasn't true.

> *"Jeanne Marie was my new love.*
> *How I loved that Jeanne Marie."*

But the war ended, and he came home, leaving her behind. I wished he'd stop falling in love. There was Bessie May, who married his best friend, and Rosalie, who married him, but ran away with his brother, and Mary Ann, who died in his arms. And more. Three ladies died in the song.

I was going to get caught because of The Song That Went On Forever.

Finally he found Sadie Lou again. He must have been at least two hundred years old, after all the girl-friends and wives he'd had. Anyway, they were happy together.

> *"Sadie Lou was my first love.*
> *How I love that Sadie Lou."*

He stopped singing.

Go back to bed. Go back to sleep.

He started the Hanukkah song, "Rock of Ages." Was he going to sing till the milkman came? I couldn't do anything. The rope was right here, but I couldn't take it and go. I started counting out minutes to see how much time was going by, but I lost track.

He finished. I heard *slish slish* again, and then sucking noises as he crossed the laundry. Then silence.

How long should I wait for him to fall asleep? I started counting again, and this time I didn't let myself lose count. After ten minutes I pulled the light cord again and stood still to listen.

I didn't hear anything, so I started wrapping the rope around my chest, under my pajama top. There was much too much. I had to cut it. I measured out the right length. There was a saw way down in the toolbox, with a hundred things on top of it. One by one, I took out the screwdriver, the hammer, several clamps, a wrench, and put them on the ground.

The chisel slipped out of my clammy fingers and landed in the dirt with a dull thud. I held my breath. Nothing happened.

I lifted out a pair of pliers and a drill, and there was the saw. But sawing the rope was going to make noise. Too much noise.

This was ridiculous. I'd taken the chance of leaving our room. I'd gotten all the way down here. Found the rope. Found the saw to cut the rope. And now I had to go back without it. Mr. Meltzer was going to catch me. He'd take me to Mr. Doom, who'd kill me, and I'd have gotten nothing out of it. I wanted to punch something, but instead I started to unwrap the rope from around my chest.

Bong. Bong.

The clock. Noise! I picked up the saw, fumbled with the rope. On the fifth bong I started sawing. The rope was tough. *Bong. Bong.* I was halfway through. *Bong.* Let it be midnight. *Bong. Bong.* The saw caught on a matted spot. *Bong. Bong.* It was through! I made it!

I put the saw back in its box and placed everything else on top of it. I wound the rope around my chest again. I was done. The coil on the floor didn't even look much smaller. I clicked off the light, edged the door open, and glided toward the laundry. Between slow, muddy steps, I stopped to listen. Ed was snoring again.

I eased the door to the stairs open. Silence. No Mr. Meltzer pounding up and down, hollering what he'd do when he laid his hands on me. So, since I'd been lucky so far, I decided to go outside and try out the rope. Why not? Mr. Meltzer could catch me now, or later, after I'd had another adventure.

But when I reached the first floor, I heard voices in the lobby. A woman was trying to dump a boy here. A prefect's voice echoed down the hall. "No admissions at night." The voice became friendlier. "But for a few bucks—"

"I don't have any money."

"I'm not getting into hot water for nothing. Sorry, lady."

She started yelling, "I can't go back . . ."

I eased the door open a crack. The kid she was trying to get rid of couldn't have been older than three. He was sitting on the floor, sucking his thumb.

"You can holler . . ."

I let the door close and waited a few minutes, but the argument went on. I started upstairs. On the second floor, I stood in front of the stairway door, too scared to open it. There was no keyhole to look through. I lay down and peered under the door. And there were Mr. Meltzer's feet, outside our room.

Why weren't they running around, looking for me?

Maybe he was waiting for me to come back. He was probably sitting there, grinning over what Mr. Doom was going to do to me.

It wasn't even one o'clock. He'd have to go to the toilet sometime. If I could get back in while he was in there . . . If I was in bed when the wake-up bell rang, he'd be confused. He wouldn't be sure I ever left. It would drive him crazy.

I waited, stretched out on the cold floor, the chill seeping into me. If the other prefect, the one in the lobby, took this staircase, he'd catch me. But there was no other choice.

The three o'clock chimes woke me. I didn't know how I could have been such a moron, to let myself sleep. Mr. Meltzer's feet were still outside our door, but he could have gone to the toilet seven times while I slept.

I tried to think of a way to make him get up, a way to make a noise he'd have to investigate that was nowhere near me. If I was a ventriloquist I could throw my voice to the other end of the hall.

Alfie started coughing. Mr. Meltzer's feet didn't move. Alfie stopped, then started again. Mr. Meltzer's feet went into our room.

Take Alfie to the nurse! Take him!

He came out with Alfie. Good. He started coming my way. Toward this staircase! Toward me!

I raced downstairs. I passed the first floor and went down half a flight more. Mr. Meltzer's footsteps marching upstairs sounded like a one-man army. I didn't hear Alfie at all. *Boom boom boom boom boom.* Then silence. I rushed upstairs and dashed into our room.

Somebody was in my bed! Harvey, fast asleep. He'd saved me! I went to his bed. Somebody was sleeping there too!

Then I looked closer, and the sleeper turned out to be a mound of clothing. I went back to my bed and shoved the rope into my suitcase. Then I ran to Harvey's bed.

Eli was sitting up. "Why didn't you tell us you were going?"

"I thought everybody was asleep." Which was true, but the real truth was, it never occurred to me to ask for help.

"You could wake us. You know we always help a buddy."

CHAPTER

20

IN THE MORNING I asked Harvey how he'd known I'd left.

"We watch out for each other, buddy," he said, which wasn't an answer.

Mike said he had heard me leave. "I knew Mr. Meltzer would check on you," he said while pulling on his earlobe. "So I woke Eli, and he told Harvey to take your place."

"I'm the right height," Harvey said.

I thanked them. Harvey could have been dragged to Mr. Doom along with me.

"Any time," Harvey said.

"Where'd you go?" Mike asked.

"Just to the basement." I told them about it. When I got to the part about the woman in the lobby, none of them thought she was dumping the kid.

"It could have been for his own good," Harvey said.

"Yeah," Eli said. "We don't know why she brought him."

"Probably he was bad," Harvey said.

How bad could he be? He wasn't more than three.

"Or maybe she was sick," Alfie said.

She was dumping him. Nothing was wrong with her.

"Or he was sick," Fred said. "And she knew we had a nurse."

"This is the last place to go if you're sick," Jeff, his twin, said. "You'd freeze to death."

Nobody said anything for a minute.

"If you go outside again," Mike said, "could you bring back some food?"

There'd be food at Irma Lee's party. I told them about it, and said I didn't know how I could go with the prefects watching me so closely. Harvey said he'd pretend to be me again if I got out.

"I'll cough till Mr. Meltzer comes and takes me to the nurse," Alfie said.

"Can you cough whenever you want to?" I asked. Maybe it wasn't consumption.

"Usually I cough because I have to." He smiled. "But I guess I could just do it, buddy."

But Alfie wasn't able to help me. He had a real coughing fit during supper, and Mr. Meltzer took him to the nurse and didn't bring him back. Then, while we were getting ready for bed, Mr. Meltzer started packing Alfie's clothes and schoolbooks into his suitcase.

"Alfie died," Mike said. He was yanking on his pajama bottoms, which were twisted and backwards.

Mr. Meltzer didn't say anything. Finally Eli asked, "What happened to Alfie?"

"They're sending him to another place. Fresh air, wholesome diet. He'll come back when he's better."

"*If* he's better," Harvey said.

"He'll die," Mike said, too soft for anybody but me to hear.

"Where is he?" Eli said. "We want to say good-bye."

"You can't. He's outside, in the doctor's car."

Eli put his pajama top on quickly. "We're going to tell him good-bye."

We all rushed to finish putting on our pajamas. I was ready, so I helped Mike get his pajama legs straightened out.

Forty boys—all of us elevens—marched through the HHB, followed by Mr. Meltzer, who yelled at us to go back to our room. We passed a couple of other prefects, who just stared.

As we walked, Mike kept saying that Alfie might not die if he was somewhere else, somewhere better than the HHB. I didn't know. My friend Morty had died of consumption, but some people got well.

The doctor's Model T was parked outside the gate. Alfie was going to get a lot of fresh air on the way to the fresh air place, because the buggy didn't have a top. He was in the backseat, and the nurse was tucking a blanket around him. When he saw us, he poked an arm out of the blanket to wave. He didn't look any worse than usual, and he wasn't even coughing. I wished we could grab him and bring him back upstairs. How did we know they were really taking him to a place that could make him better? Places like that had to be expensive, and I didn't think anybody would spend much on an orphan.

"The doctor says they have horseback riding upstate, where I'm going. But I may not—" He started coughing.

The nurse closed the door, and the car drove away. Alfie waved and coughed while we yelled good-bye and hollered that he was getting a good deal, that those horses better watch out, and that he should get fat and bring food back for the rest of us.

Later, in bed, I thought about Papa and Alfie mixed up together. I thought about how people seemed to vanish when they died. It felt as though Papa had disappeared, even though I saw him go into the ground. And now Alfie had vanished, even though he hadn't died. Not yet, anyway. Alfie was a whole, like me, and nobody ever came to see him on Visiting Day either. He didn't have any brothers or sisters to miss him if he died, not even a deserting rat of a brother. Well, we'd miss him. His buddies would miss him.

Then I got mad at myself for thinking of him as already dead when he'd probably be back in a few weeks with roses in his cheeks.

I rolled over and tried to fall asleep. I felt so tired, like my bones were turning to icy jelly. If Papa's carving

had been sitting on the floor five feet away from my bed
I wouldn't have been able to stand up and get it.

And then I remembered Irma Lee's party. I had forgotten about it in the commotion over Alfie. Well, I
couldn't go. I couldn't get out with Mr. Meltzer on
duty, and I didn't feel like trying. I was sorry I couldn't
tell her why I couldn't come. But I wasn't sorry I
couldn't go. The last thing I wanted was a party.

The lump in my throat was the size of an orange.
I wished I could cry, but I couldn't. It was too cold to
cry anyway. My tears would freeze. I stared down at
the tiled floor. I hated everything. Mike was making a
racket in the next bed, and I hated him for being so
noisy. I hated Danny for snoring. I hated Alfie for leaving. I hated Papa for dying. I hated myself for being an
orphan, for being cold, for not being able to fall asleep.

The next thing I knew, somebody was shaking me
awake. I opened my eyes. It was Mr. Meltzer.

I was terrified. There'd been a telegram. Gideon was
dead. I could tell from the breathing around me that my
buddies were awake. Mike was unusually still.

"What?" I whispered.

"Get dressed."

I was right. It was a telegram.

I had trouble getting my knickers on. Finally I was
dressed. I followed Mr. Meltzer out.

Solly and Bandit were in the hall.

"Tell for you your fortune?" the parrot squawked.

CHAPTER 21

SOLLY EXPLAINED AS we walked toward Convent Avenue. It was cold out, just like it was in. But I was warm because Mr. Meltzer had given me somebody's winter coat and somebody's cap to wear.

The air was crisp and fresh. I wanted to run or skip, but Solly didn't walk very fast. He said he had told Mr. Meltzer he was my grandpa. "I said your cousin had just gotten married, and they wanted you at the party. I could see I had to shmeer him, so I slipped him a dollar. The nebbish almost kissed me. From him I could have gotten you out for a quarter."

A dollar! I walked along, thinking about it. He'd spent a lot on me at the rent party too, paying for me to get in and giving me a dollar at the end. "How did you find me?" I asked, trying to understand.

"You think I can't learn what an HHB is, boychik?"

The parrot squawked, "Boychik!"

Solly was the nicest grown-up I'd run into in a long time. He knew how much I wanted to go to Irma Lee's party, so, when I didn't show up where we were supposed to meet, he came and got me. "Thanks," I said and repeated, "Thanks."

"Think nothing of it."

It was swell, being out and not having to worry about getting caught. Mr. Meltzer would be waiting for us at five-thirty. Solly said it was twelve-thirty now, so we had hours.

"Do you have any real grandchildren?" Maybe I reminded him of a dead son or grandson.

"My son, the alrightnik, has three little alrightniks. A girl and two boys. One boy wants to be a banker. The other boy wants to own a factory. My granddaughter, Heloise—what kind of a name is Heloise?—wants a pearl necklace for her birthday. Nine years old, and she wants pearls."

They didn't sound like kids who'd help their grandpa be a gonif. "I'm going to run away from the HHB," I announced.

"Tonight? I promised that nebbish—"

"Not tonight. After I do something."

We were going around Saint Nicholas Park. That was the name of the park I'd gone through before, when I went to the rent party. Solly was afraid he'd trip and fall if we walked through it.

I took a deep breath. "Could I stay with you after I run away?"

"You think this is a good idea, bubeleh?"

"I could help you. I could groan. You said—"

"You *could* help me. I'm an old man. I could use a little help. But they'd never let me adopt you. An old—"

"You wouldn't have—"

"An old man without a job. They wouldn't believe that being a gonif is full-time work."

"You wouldn't have to adopt me."

"So? How would you go to school? They'd—"

"I wouldn't have to go—"

"What if you got sick and I had to take you—"

"I'm healthy. I wouldn't get—"

"What if *I* got sick? Nu?"

I stopped arguing. He didn't want me, and he had a million excuses for it. Just like my relatives. I took it back, about him being so nice. He probably had a reason for coming for me, which I'd figure out sooner or later. Well, it didn't matter about staying with him. I'd find a place whether he helped or not.

"Slow down a little, boychik. My legs are a lot older than yours."

I waited, tapping my foot. He was shuffling along so slowly that by the time we got to the party, we'd have to leave again. Cars honked far away, but these streets were silent. A few parked cars, no swanky ones.

Everything woke up, though, once we crossed under the el at Eighth Avenue. People were in the streets, most of them colored. Lots of cars, lots of honking. We turned onto Seventh Avenue. Most of the stores were still open. We passed a pharmacy and a shoe store. A pair of Florsheim shoes in the window cost eight dollars and eighty-five cents. Ida would have screamed highway robbery. She wouldn't have paid more than six.

"Why are those stores open in the middle of the night?" I asked before I remembered I was mad.

"Drugstores-shmugstores, shoe stores–shmoo stores— they all sell the same merchandise. *Especially* at night."

They were selling liquor! I laughed to myself. My friend Ben and I used to play Cops and Bootleggers. But our games never had anything to do with shoe stores or drugstores.

Between 131st and 132nd Streets a knot of dressed-up white people stood under an awning, waiting to enter a building with a yellow door, a nightclub or speakeasy, most likely. We had to step off the curb to get around them.

A few steps beyond the awning, I heard someone calling Solly.

"Hey, fortune-teller. Hey, Solly. Wait up."

It was Martin, the trumpet player from the rent party. He said he was playing at a club called the Exclusive, and then he was going to a rent party on 142nd Street.

"Catch you later, Solly?"

"Not tonight. Tonight we're mingling at Odelia Packer's."

Martin whistled. "You're going to work the crowd at Odelia's?"

Solly shook his head. "Tonight the boychik and I are members of the leisure class."

That was the reason he got me out of the HHB. So he could go to the party. He knew that Irma Lee had only invited him because she wanted me to come. He wanted to meet rich people he could sell fortunes to.

Solly went on. "Don't I look like a member of the leisure class?" He stood still.

He wasn't wearing an overcoat. He had on the same baggy black suit as last time, the same beat-up gray hat, the same wrinkled white shirt, and a different ugly tie. No, wait. There was a wilted daisy in his lapel. He looked more bedraggled than ever.

Martin laughed. "You look like the bee's knees." He laughed harder. "The butterfly's boots. Man, you look like the elephant's eyebrows."

"Thank you." Solly started walking again, finally.

Martin left us at 133rd Street. I started worrying that Irma Lee might not remember me. "I think we should go to that rent party," I said. "Don't you need the money?"

"Money-shmoney. Tonight is a night you'll tell your grandchildren about. Maybe your real grandchildren, or maybe a grandchild you find on the street, swiping dollar bills."

I didn't swipe the dollar. It had fallen out a window. I wasn't like him. I hadn't tricked the money out of people's wallets.

He continued. "All the big shots go to Odelia's if they can. Once even the prince of Sweden couldn't get in." Solly chuckled. "But Odelia sent a bottle of champagne out to him to drink on the street."

Prince-shmince. The sultan of Turkey once gave my papa a medal.

We turned onto 134th Street. The street was clogged with cars. A Cadillac, a Packard, a Doble—a steam-powered car!, a Lincoln, and two—two!—Pierce-Arrows!

Irma Lee's house was built of reddish stone. It was three stories tall, and I wondered if it all belonged to Mrs. Packer. Above the four long windows on the first floor were smaller ones made of stained glass. A green-and-white-striped awning hung over the double wooden doors, and a flight of stone steps went from the doors down to the sidewalk, which was crowded with colored people and white people all dressed up, holding glasses and plates of food. A maid, a white lady in a black dress with a white ruffly apron, walked through the crowd, carrying a silver tray with tiny pies on it.

"Tell for you your fortune?" Bandit squawked.

People turned to look at us and then turned away again. A tall colored lady came toward us.

"Solly! You can't get away from me now."

"Dora, the meshuggeneh!"

Meshuggeneh means a crazy person. But Solly was smiling.

Dora reached into the pocket of the loose jacket she wore over a very short dress. She pulled out a tape measure and started measuring Solly's head. He let her. The parrot flapped its wings.

"Watch out, Bandit," she said, laughing, "or I'll do your head next."

"He's a smart bird," Solly said.

"Very interesting." She pulled a notebook out of her pocket and wrote Solly's measurements in it. "Your head is especially wide and flat."

"Nu? This is important?"

"It could be. Can I do the boy?"

"So ask him."

She turned to me. "May I?"

"Okay."

But she didn't start measuring. "I'm Dora. Are you a writer?"

I shook my head.

"Thank heavens. Another writer, and the gravity at this party would sink us all twenty feet under."

"I'm an artist," I said. "I do gesture and line drawings."

She groaned. "That's almost as bad. Let's see if you have an artist's head." She started measuring.

"Pardon me."

Dora took the tape measure off my head and turned. It was the maid. "Are you Mr. Dave?" she asked.

Nobody ever called me mister before. "I guess so."

"And you're Mr. Solly?"

"And this is Mr. Bandit."

"Come with me. Miss Irma Lee has been expecting you."

CHAPTER 22

I SAID GOOD-BYE to Dora and followed the maid
through the crowd outside the door. A strip of
flowered carpet ran from the curb, across the
sidewalk, and up the steps to Irma Lee's door.

The maid pushed open a glossy wooden door. Inside,
it was as crowded as Hester Street in my old neighborhood. The maid waited while I unbuttoned my coat.
Then she helped me take it off. This was the leisure
class!

The maid put the coat and my cap over her arm and
headed into the crowd. Solly put his hands on my shoulders. I wished I could hang on to the maid. I wouldn't
have minded losing Solly, but I didn't want to lose her.

The parrot squawked, "Oy vay!"

I heard snatches of conversation.

"Did you read it?" Woman's voice.

"*Fire!!* is the right word for it." Man's voice.

"I think I see a bird." Another man's voice.

Beyond the voices I heard sweet, tinkly music. The maid was disappearing ahead of us. People made room for her, but not for us. We inched forward, but she was gone.

"It won't be the first time a vulture came to Odelia's." A different woman's voice.

"This bird's a parrot."

The people in front of me separated, and there was the maid again. She took my hand. "Stay right behind me."

The crowd still let her through but not us. Her grip on my hand was like iron. She's going to pull my arm off, I thought. When she finds Irma Lee that's all she'll have of me.

Behind me, Solly chanted, "Coming through. Announcing the crown prince of Spain. Make way."

Bandit squawked, "Mazel tov, boychik. Oy vay."

I put my shoulders back, lifted my chin, and tried to look like the crown prince of Spain, whoever he was.

They let us through. In a little while the crowd thinned. Fewer people, but a million books. The walls were filled with them. At the end of the room, a colored woman played a grand piano and a white man played a harp. If the music at the rent party was pot roast gravy—tasty and rich—this was seltzer—light, bubbly, nothing-to-it music.

The maid faced us. "Miss Irma Lee only asked to see Mr. Dave."

See? I was right.

"What would she want with an old man anyway? But tell me, girly, where's Odelia? I want to pay my respects."

"Mrs. Packer is in the card room."

"So where's the card room?"

"Follow me, both of you."

The next room was the living room. There was a circular couch with seats facing out. In the middle, behind your head if you were sitting on the couch, a mahogany stand held a huge vase of ferns. Way above the ferns was a chandelier with at least a thousand dangling pieces of glass. There was a big mirror with mahogany columns on each side of it. Solly and I looked pretty shabby as we walked by.

> *Irma Lee was my first love.*
> *How I loved my Irma Lee.*
> *But I was a poor boy,*
> *And she had a rich family.*

Next was the dining room. A table filled the room, and food filled the table. I saw a whole turkey, half eaten, an enormous roast beef, a basket bursting with rolls. My stomach rumbled. A sideboard was covered with cakes. I remembered my promise to bring food back to my buddies.

The maid opened an oak door leading to a back stairway grand enough to be the front one. Solly was out of breath before he'd taken four steps.

Would Irma Lee be as perfect as I remembered? Would she still want to be friends?

The wallpaper in the second-floor hallway was dark red and gold. Big paintings in golden frames hung on the walls. The lighting was too dim to see them well. The first room we passed was the toilet. A toilet in your own house. Not in the hall, shared with Mr. and Mrs. Stern and their five children and their two boarders, plus our boarders, when we had them. I peeked inside. It had a bathtub!

The maid opened the door to the next room, which turned out to be the card room. The air was foggy from cigarette smoke. Mrs. Packer sat at a table with a white man and two colored women. A few more people sat on a couch or stood talking in front of the window.

Mrs. Packer smiled. "Solly, sit with me and bring me mazel. Dave, my baby's been looking for you ever since she woke up this morning."

The maid and I left. She led me past three doors to the last room on the right. Inside, Irma Lee was on the floor playing jacks. The ball dribbled across the floor away from her. She jumped up and smiled at me.

She was even prettier than I remembered. She sparkled like a new penny, like the sun on water.

The maid left and closed the door behind her.

"Dave! I thought you weren't coming. Did you and Mr. Gruber have to sneak away from your mama again?"

My voice wouldn't work right. "Unhh."

She laughed. "Do you know how to play jacks?"

I shook my head.

"Where'd that ball go?"

I looked around. There it was, stuck under one rocker of a rocking horse. I pointed.

The horse was practically big enough to be on a carousel. The room was big too, as big as our old apartment. Only our apartment didn't have windows that went from the floor to the ceiling, or a radiator for heat, or a round rug next to the bed. And Papa's bed didn't have a carved and upholstered headboard.

Leaning against the wall behind the rocking horse was a pair of stilts. A doll with blond hair and a lacy dress rested on a pile of pillows on Irma Lee's bed. An enormous dollhouse stood on a table in front of a window. Against the wall across from Irma Lee's bed was a piano. Two pianos in one house!

Irma Lee picked up the ball. She tugged me down onto the wooden floor. "I'll teach you." She gathered up the jacks and tossed them out. "Watch. I do ones first. They're easy."

She threw the ball into the air. Her skirt was short, and I saw a scab on her left knee. Her socks were light green like her dress, and a red flower was embroidered above the ankle. She picked up a jack as the ball bounced and then caught the ball with the same hand. The way she caught it was just right—nothing extra.

"Could I draw a picture of you?" I didn't mean to say that, and my heart started banging away.

She spun toward me, scattering jacks. "Are you an artist, Dave Caros?"

I shrugged. "I want to be," I muttered.

She sprang to her feet. She never stayed still for more than a second—she was almost as jumpy as Mike.

"You want crayons? Or chalk? I have colored chalk, and I have paint too."

"Crayons."

She got crayons and a pad out of a toy chest at the foot of her bed. "What should I do?" She stood on one foot in front of me.

I decided to draw her doing something, because she always was. "We learned to do these gesture drawings in school." I told her about them. Then I said, "Could you, um, twirl around, and when I say 'stop' stay very still?"

She twirled around twice, and when she got back to me the second time, I told her to stop. She stopped suddenly, her skirt settling slowly. She stood with her arms out for balance, leaning on one foot with the other one behind her.

"Can you stay like that?"

She didn't nod or say anything, she just didn't move. I sat on the floor. It was a grand pose, exactly right for her.

I only used the black crayon, the way we had in class. I started light, because I was afraid of making a mistake. Irma Lee's drawing pad was too small, but I tried to draw big anyway, to fill the page, the way Mr. Hillinger had shown us.

I marked her in, making her head bigger than it was and the rest of her smaller. I wanted to show how she reminded me of a flower, trying to get the sun. But it didn't work. It made her look like a dwarf with a big head. I crumpled up the page.

She didn't move anything except her eyes, watching me drop the wadded-up paper.

I started over. I shaded around the back of her head and the top side of her left arm, putting in a line where the doorway met her shoulder. Draw all around the page, I reminded myself. I shaded the floor around the leg she was leaning on. She stayed completely still, even though I was taking too long.

I drew her skirt, not the space around it. Then I did the space around her other arm and the side of her face. She still didn't budge.

It was going well. You could tell she had just been twirling. I was afraid to do her face, but she had to have one. Mr. Hillinger had said to have courage. I made a light smudge where her mouth should go and put in a little shadow under her cheeks. Maybe that was enough. No. She needed a face. I started to outline her left eye.

It was too high up, and it spoiled everything. Maybe I could try—

The door opened. Irma Lee spun around. Mrs. Packer came in. She'd see the botched-up face in the drawing. Irma Lee would too. I turned the pad face-down and put it on the floor. Then I stood up.

CHAPTER

23

"MAMA!" IRMA LEE sounded furious. "You said you'd—"

"Now, baby gi—"

"I'm not a baby!"

"I know, sugar. I just came up here to say hi and make sure you two were enjoying yourselves. Baby—honey, did you take Dave to get something to eat?"

Irma Lee turned to me, looking worried.

"Irma Lee asked me," I lied, "but I had a big supper before I came." I hoped they'd forget about the drawing.

"Were you drawing my baby girl?"

I shrugged. I didn't want her to see the drawing with one eye halfway up the forehead.

Mrs. Packer didn't make me turn the pad over. She just said, "Be sure to introduce Dave to Aaron

Douglas if he comes, baby girl."

"In a little while, Mama. You said—"

"All right, babe— sweetheart. I'm going back to my game. You know where I am if you need me." She closed the door behind her, leaving a heavy perfumed scent in the room.

"Let me see my picture."

"I messed up your face." I didn't bend down for it.

She didn't look. Instead, she plunked herself down on the floor. "If you could have one wish, what would it be?"

For Papa to be alive again.

This was the time to tell her I was an orphan. I sat down and slid the drawing pad behind me. "Solly isn't my grandpa."

"Then why are you pretending?" She didn't sound mad at me for lying, just curious. "And what about your mama and sneaking out in your pajamas?"

I picked up one of the jacks and turned it over and over in my hand. I couldn't look at her while I told the truth. "I snuck out of the HHB, the orphanage, in my pajamas. My mama's dead."

She didn't say anything, so I kept talking and looking at the jack. "My papa died six and a half weeks ago, and my wish would be for him to be alive."

I looked up. Tears were rolling down her cheeks. She didn't need to cry over me. I was all right. But maybe she was crying about her own parents too.

"When did your mama die?" she asked.

I told her how Mama died because of me, and then I found myself describing Papa's carving, because she was in it. While I talked, she stopped crying.

"Can you sneak out whenever you want to?"

"I can get out sometimes."

"Could you bring the carving to show me?"

I shook my head. "Mr. Doom has it." I told her about the things in my suitcase and seeing the carving in his knickknack cabinet. I didn't mention him beating me. "But I'm going to get the carving away from him."

"How?"

"I don't know, but I am."

She got up on her knees and collected the jacks and the ball. "This is how you do the twos."

"What would your wish be?" I asked.

"To go to school and jump rope and play tag and have girlfriends."

I stared. "You don't go to school?"

She shook her head.

"Do you know how to read?" I could teach her.

She jumped up and pulled a book out of the bookcase against the wall. "This was written by a friend of Mama's." She shifted her feet so she was standing straighter. Then she coughed and began. "'The Weary Blues' by Langston Hughes.

"*Droning a drowsy syncopated tune,*
   Rocking back and forth to a mellow croon,
      I heard a Negro play.

Down on Lenox Avenue the other night
By the pale dull pallor of an old gas light
He did a lazy sway . . .
He did a lazy sway . . .
To the tune o' those Weary Blues."

She read it slowly. When she said *sway*, she dragged it out, so I felt the musician sway. And when she said *weary*, she sounded weary. I clapped.

She looked embarrassed. "Miss Mulready teaches me to declaim, and all my other subjects. She comes every day."

"Why don't you go to school?" I wished I didn't have to.

"Mama likes to keep me nearby, and she—"

The door opened again. Irma Lee swung around. "Darn it! Ma—"

But it was Solly. "So, boychik, here you are." He sat on Irma Lee's bed.

I stood, picking up the drawing pad and holding it behind me.

"Mr. Gruber," Irma Lee said, "would you tell my fortune?"

"Tell for you your fortune?" the parrot squawked.

If he tried to trick her, I'd tell her he was a phony.

"Irmaleh, my fortunes aren't the gontzeh megillah, the whole story."

Good. He knew better with me watching.

"I don't care."

Solly took the cards out of his pocket and shuffled them. Behind my back, I tore the drawing off the pad. Then I turned away from Solly and Irma Lee, folded it up, and stuffed it into the waist of my knickers.

"The boychik can help me."

While Solly shuffled the cards, I rocked, moaning softly with my eyes almost closed. Irma Lee giggled.

Solly turned a card over on the bed. A nine of hearts. "When you're nine years old you will get married."

Irma Lee giggled harder. "I'm ten and a half."

"So I made a mistake."

I groaned loudly.

Solly turned over another card and placed it to the left of the nine. It was a five. "The cards tell all. When you are fifty-nine you will get married."

"For the first time?"

Solly turned over another card. "For the sixth time. Or you will have six children. The cards are not clear."

"Or I'll have five hundred and ninety-six children."

"Not possible," Solly said. "I would never prophesy such a thing." He turned over a joker.

"Is that my husband?"

"You're planning on marrying a playing card, Irmaleh?" He gathered up the cards. "I came in to see if my grandson wants to get something to eat."

Irma Lee whirled on me. "You didn't eat before you came, did you?"

I shrugged. "Irma Lee knows you're not my grandpa." He could tell his own lies.

"That's right. You shouldn't lie to your friends." He stood up. "So, let's go eat."

Irma Lee led us to the front staircase, which was much grander than the back one. The three of us could walk down it side by side, and the carpet was so deep it practically tickled my ankles.

Halfway down, Solly grabbed my arm. "Look, boychik." I could barely hear him. The crowd was even thicker than before. And the noise was a roar, louder than a subway train.

Solly talked right into my ear. "See the bald-headed colored man with the goatee?" He pointed.

Hurry up, I thought. I'm hungry. "Uh-huh." I did see him. There was a little space around him.

"That's W. E. B. Du Bois. A scholar and a writer for the Negroes. A genius."

Someone at the bottom of the stairs called to Irma Lee, and she went down without us. I was afraid of losing her, but Solly was still clutching my arm.

"And look." He pointed at a colored man coming through the door. "That's Caspar Holstein, a big crook."

"Like you?"

"A gonif is a big crook like a mouse is a mountain lion. That no-goodnik runs the numbers game in Harlem. I, on the other hand, only . . . Ahhh . . . Ahhh. And do you see, Dave, that bunch, the ones laughing with Dora?"

I nodded.

"They're all poets and writers, colored poets and

writers. Tell your grandchildren you saw Countee Cullen, Wallace Thurman, Arna Bontemps, Langston Hughes—they won't believe you. You'll see."

Langston Hughes wrote the poem Irma Lee had read to me. It was interesting to see him. I'd never been in the same place before with someone whose words were in a book. But I didn't want to stand still, staring at him. I wanted to get back to Irma Lee.

She was only a little way into the crowd, talking to a hat. Not really, but that's what it looked like from up here. The lady was wearing a purple hat—another fishbowl-shaped one. I couldn't see her face at all. Solly finally let go of me, and I ran down the stairs.

"Irma Lee . . ." I said.

She excused herself from the lady. "There's foie gras and oysters," she shouted to me. "Come on."

Solly caught up with me and put his hands on my shoulders. "Make way for the crown prince and princess of Sheba."

Irma Lee was about to disappear ahead of us. I lunged forward and put my hands on her shoulders. Her dress felt smooth and soft, and I could feel her bones underneath.

"Make way for the crown prince and princess of Sheba."

The crowd parted.

CHAPTER
24

$\mathcal{T}$HE DINING ROOM was crowded and noisy, but not as bad as the hall. I could hear the pianist and the harpist playing two rooms away.

I didn't know what a lot of the food was. I'd never seen an oyster before or a snail or the tiny slippery things Irma Lee said were fish eggs. I'd gladly have shared any of them with Moe. They were slimy.

But I liked the foie gras, which tasted like chopped liver. And I liked the roast beef and the turkey and the stuffing and the leg of lamb and the creamed potatoes and the sweet-as-sugar baked carrots. I even liked the strange salad—banana slices and popcorn mixed together on a big lettuce leaf with dabs of goo on top that Irma Lee said was mayonnaise.

Some people in the corner called to Irma Lee to join them. She made a face, but she went. I didn't mind. I wanted to concentrate on eating. After I finished big helpings of everything, I went back for more. Solly had said nobody would care. He'd said they'd throw the leftovers away, but I didn't believe him.

As I ate, I walked over to the painting that hung over the sideboard. I swallowed hard and stared. The painting was of Noah's ark! But a completely different version from Papa's. In this version the storm had already begun. Looking at it, you knew you were watching an emergency. There were lightning flashes, even though a hazy sun still shone. From the deck of the ark, a Negro Noah raised his arm and gave orders. The two animals climbing into the ark were marching in double time. The only colors were pale purples and pale greens, and the drawing was simple, but there was nothing wrong with that. The painting felt powerful. I ate slowly, following the direction of the shapes with my eyes and trying to figure out how the artist had done everything.

The signature was A. Douglas. Aaron Douglas. Mrs. Packer had said he might be here tonight. I turned around, looking for Irma Lee. If Mr. Douglas was here I wanted to ask him why he used such pale colors. But she wasn't in the room anymore, and neither was Mrs. Packer and the people they had been talking to.

I put my plate down on the buffet table, meaning to look for Irma Lee. But then I thought this was a good time to stock up on food for my buddies.

It wasn't stealing, not if they were going to throw

the leftovers away. Well, maybe it was, but it was gonif stealing, not big-crook stealing.

If only I had more pockets. There were none in my jacket or my shirt, and the two in my knickers wouldn't hold much. I unbuttoned two buttons on my shirt near the waistband of my knickers. You could hardly tell my shirt was open, because of the folded drawing, which was white too. I took a roll and glanced around. Nobody was watching. Through the doorway I saw Solly two rooms away, looking at the books.

I slipped the roll inside my shirt and pushed it toward the back, where the jacket would cover the bulge. But one roll would be a crumb for each eleven. What else could I take?

There was a plate with chunks of carrot and celery on it. It wouldn't be their favorite food, but it wouldn't squoosh. I took a handful. The vegetables would fit in my pockets.

"It's so unusual to see a child who likes his vegetables."

I turned. A light-skinned colored lady with gray hair smiled at me.

I bit into a carrot and smiled back. "Mmm. Yum." The music in the next room stopped just then, and my voice was too loud. I lowered it and added, "Delicious and good for me."

"I love carrots too." She took one and chomped on it. "Who's your daddy, son?"

"Abraham Caros. But I'm here with my grandpa, Solly Gruber."

"He must be proud of you."

For eating vegetables? "I guess he is."

We stood there, smiling at each other. Then she gave a little laugh. "Well. Excuse me. I have to find my husband." She took another carrot and headed into the crowd.

I stuffed the vegetables into my pockets. Then I saw a platter of fruit and a bowl of nuts on the sideboard with the cakes and pies and cookies. I grabbed an apple and looked around. Nobody was paying attention. I shoved it into the back of my shirt.

That man, across the table—was he watching me? His head was tilted, listening to another man. But his eyes were on me. I smiled at him and waved, but his expression didn't change. I stuck my fingers in the corners of my mouth, pulled back, and stuck my tongue out. His expression still didn't change. He wasn't really seeing me. I took another apple, and then another. They settled around my waist. It was a good thing my shirt was too big. I looked around again, took a handful of nuts, and added them to my collection.

Above the sideboard was a mirror. I turned sideways and looked to see if the fruit and vegetables made my jacket stick out. They didn't.

Enough. I buttoned my shirt and cut myself a slice of chocolate cake. Irma Lee came back in with a tall Negro man. I walked toward them, carrying my plate and eating. The food in my shirt jiggled. "Is Mr. Doug—"

At the exact same moment she said, "Can you—"

We laughed, and the man said, "Let the boy talk, Irma Lee."

So I asked if Mr. Aaron Douglas was at the party, and she said he hadn't come. Then she said, "Can you Charleston, Dave Caros?"

"I'll dance with you," the man said.

"You're too big, Mr. Johnson. I want to dance with Dave."

The man laughed. "I'm too old, you mean."

"There's no mu—"

At that moment, the piano in the next room started playing again, but it wasn't light and tinkly anymore. It was like the music at the rent party, what Solly called jazz. A drum joined the piano. Irma Lee grabbed my hand and tugged me toward the music.

"I don't know how to dance." And I couldn't dance with fruit and nuts in my shirt.

A trumpet started singing. It zigged and zagged above the piano and the drums.

"Come on."

The room with the musicians was mobbed, and everybody was dancing.

"It's the Charleston," Irma Lee shouted and started doing it too, arms and legs flying, grinning and laughing.

I didn't know what to do. I just stood there. Irma

Lee stopped dancing and stopped grinning. I couldn't spoil things for her. I put my left hand behind my back to hold the food, threw my right arm around wildly, and started jumping up and down. It made Irma Lee laugh, and she started going again.

The apples kept bumping into my back, and the roll was probably squashed, and the nuts were scratchy—but they all stayed where they were supposed to.

The music got inside me. It felt like my bones were humming and bouncing along. I tried to imitate Irma Lee. She pointed her right toe and both her arms went to the right, her right arm went way up in the air. When she brought her foot in, her arms went the other way, but not as far. Then she stuck her left foot out behind her, arched her back, and sent her arms way off to the right again. And she did it all while jumping and skipping.

I couldn't do it. Sure, I could point my toe and hop and bring my free hand up. But I couldn't do them all at once in time to the music.

Never mind. I'd just go on making it up. I kicked up my feet. Irma Lee laughed harder. I swung my arm around and around like a propeller and kicked my feet out behind me like I was trying to keep from falling. It seemed right with what the drums were doing. I kicked my feet out side to side and waved my arms over my head.

And the man dancing next to me crashed into me,

and I went down, and my shirt came out of my knickers and the vegetables came out of my pockets. The apples rolled around on the floor, and people started slipping on nuts and carrots and celery. And the song ended and the music stopped.

CHAPTER 25

a WOMAN ALMOST fell on top of me, but her partner caught her.

Irma Lee said, "What happened? Where . . ." And then she looked at me, and she knew.

I wanted to evaporate. I wanted to turn myself into somebody else. Somebody like Gideon, who would never get into this kind of trouble. I wanted to turn time back an hour, before this started, and do it over. I wanted most of all not to cry.

A maid came from someplace and started sweeping up. I reached into my shirt and pulled out a few nuts and the crushed roll. I held them out to her. There was no point in trying to hide anything now.

Irma Lee started laughing. "You look . . . so . . . funny!" she gasped.

She was laughing at me. She knew I was a thief and thought I was an idiot.

She was right.

"The squashed . . . roll . . . the—"

A man interrupted. "It's not funny. Whites always steal from us, although they usually do it sneakier."

Irma Lee tried to stop laughing. "He didn't steal." A giggle got out. "It was for our picnic in the backyard." Then she was off laughing again. "Celery . . . in . . . your hair . . . Your shirt . . ."

A few other people joined the laughter. Then the music started up, and everybody went back to dancing.

She'd stuck up for me! She thought it was funny. She was crazy—good crazy—the best crazy!

I was still on the floor. The maid picked up the last celery stick. All around me people were dancing. I guess it *was* funny. I thought of Papa, what he'd think of this mess. He'd laugh. He'd roar.

I stood up and jumped around again in time to the music. Before I left tonight, I was going to make sure she knew I had stolen for my buddies, not for myself.

She started dancing too. She danced next to me and tried to get me to learn the Charleston. By the end of the song I'd caught on a little, even though my arms kept going the wrong way.

In the quiet after the song ended, Irma Lee asked, "You want to see the backyard where we were going to have a picnic?"

"Okay."

She took my hand again. It was so friendly and trusting when she did that. I followed her through the dining room and into the kitchen, where a woman was taking another roast out of the oven, and a man was washing dishes. Beyond the kitchen was a small room lined with shelves full of cans and jars. Facing us was the door to the backyard.

We went out. The cold air felt good. Irma Lee flicked a switch on the door frame, and a light came on. The yard was only as wide as the house and not very deep. But it was crammed with things, mostly statues of men and women, some of them naked. There was a statue of a horse, as big as a horse. And there were statues of heads, just heads, with their necks and a bit of their shoulders. They looked like they were growing out of the ground, like somebody had planted head seeds. There were also two benches and some dried-up plants left over from the summer.

"The food was for my buddies at the orphanage."

"Why did you put it all in your shirt?"

"Because my pockets weren't big enough." I started laughing again. It sounded so silly.

Irma Lee laughed too. "I can give you better food to take back."

I couldn't walk in with a platter. "It has to be something I can sneak in."

"All right. I'll give you a loaf of potato bread."

It was eerie out here. The light was dim, and the statues by the back fence were just shadowy shapes.

"We could play hide-and-seek," I said. "There are lots of good hiding places."

Irma Lee looked so happy it was like I had given her a million dollars and she needed a million dollars—which she didn't. "Should I hide, or do you want to?" she asked.

"I'll hide." If she hid I'd never find her. She'd know all the best places.

She leaned against the house and started counting. I stood next to a statue of a man shooting an arrow and imitated him. Irma Lee might not notice me.

"Fifty-nine, sixty, sixty-one . . ."

Nothing was big enough to hide me completely. I ended up crawling under a bench.

"Ninety-nine, a hundred." She turned and started searching for me with her eyes, not moving. But she didn't look low enough. She moved away from home base. When she was farther away from it than I was, I began to inch out. She didn't see me. I scrambled the rest of the way out. But before I could even stand up, she was tagging me and laughing.

There she was, laughing down at me. So close, so close. I stood up and kissed her cheek. Her skin felt soft and smooth and *nice*. Then I backed away. I couldn't believe I'd done it.

She went on laughing. "You're it. I caught you, Dave Caros."

I blurted, "I'm going to run away from the Home

after I get my carving back. Do you know any place I could stay?"

She didn't stop to think. "You could stay in our basement." She nodded. "You really could. Mama never goes down there. I'd bring you food. I could bring pillows down to make you a . . ."

That was a friend! She could be an honorary buddy, except for being a girl.

I had a place to stay. Now all I needed was the carving.

"I could teach you what Miss Mulready teaches me. I could teach you to play jacks. And to do the Charleston better. And the Black Bottom. We could jump rope."

Jacks and jumping rope were for girls, but I guessed I could do it.

"You could come upstairs when Mama's not home."

"Could I get out sometimes?" I asked.

"Sure. And you could meet Solly and go to rent parties . . . When are you coming?"

"Soon. As soon as I get Papa's carving back."

The door opened and Solly came out. He was out of breath, and the parrot was flapping its wings. "I climbed almost to the roof, looking for you. We'd better leave, or I'll turn into a pumpkin and the nebbish won't let you in."

I smiled at him. It didn't matter anymore that he wouldn't let me stay with him. I liked him again. After all, he did go through trouble and expense to get me out of the HHB tonight.

Before we left, Irma Lee gave me the loaf of potato bread, which weighed at least ten pounds. It was big, but I could sneak it in under my jacket.

"Mr. Gruber," she said after she gave me the bread, "are you going to bring Dave to any more parties?"

"Could be, Irmaleh. He's a good groaner."

"Good-bye," I said.

We shook hands.

She whispered to me, "I'll get everything ready. Hurry up and get your carving back."

CHAPTER
26

IT WAS STILL dark out, and music still drifted from some of the windows on Seventh Avenue. When ever we heard a snatch of jazz music, Solly stopped to listen.

It would be swell, living in Irma Lee's basement, having fun with her, and being a gonif with Solly. Plus getting enough to eat and not going to school. And then I thought, What about my buddies? What about Mr. Hillinger's classes? I shook my head. I was leaving the HHB.

"So, Daveleh. Did you like being in high society?"

"Uh-huh. Are you going to any rent parties soon?" We turned the corner of 127th Street and Saint Nicholas Avenue, where Saint Nicholas Park started.

"Almost every night I go. It's my business."

"Where will you be tomorrow? I mean, today." It was morning already.

"I don't know so far in advance."

The same day was too far in advance? "When will you know?"

"Tonight."

"So, nu?" I said. "Can I come with you?"

"When will you sleep, boychik? Me, I have all day to nap."

I felt wide awake and ready for a game of stickball. "I'm not tired."

"Daveleh, why don't you stay safe and sound in your HHB?"

Safe and sound and cold and hungry. I didn't answer. Solly waited and then said, "Meaning you'll do what you want, never mind what I say?" He sighed. "Better you should be with a responsible gonif. Listen, boychik. Tonight you'll sleep. Tomorrow night you'll meet me at the Tree of Hope."

What was that? A speakeasy? "What is it?"

"It sounds biblical, doesn't it, Daveleh?"

"Is it a real tree?"

"What else would it be? Musicians go there, and people looking for musicians hire them there. And I go there too."

Oh. That's how he found out about rent parties. "Where is it?"

"The Tree of Hope is on Seventh Avenue and a Hundred and Thirty-second Street. We passed it on the way to the party. You didn't notice?"

I shook my head.

"Suppose I wait for you from twelve to one. Is that good?"

I nodded. "Thanks." I wished I had a watch. I'd have to listen for the chimes.

"If you don't come Monday, I'll wait Tuesday. If a week goes by and no boychik, I'll shlep to the HHB and shmeer the nebbish again. What's a little money to a rich man like me?"

We were five minutes late getting back to the orphanage. Mr. Meltzer was mad till Solly gave him another shmeer, a quarter "for his trouble." Then Mr. Meltzer smiled, which almost cracked his face into splinters.

As I followed Mr. Meltzer down the halls, I thought how bare and dead the Hollow Home for Boys was compared to Irma Lee's jumping party.

But our room came alive as soon as the door shut behind Mr. Meltzer.

"I thought you were gone for good," Mike said.

"Where would he go?" Harvey said.

Irma Lee's basement. That's where.

"Did somebody die?" Mike asked. "One of your relatives?"

"No. Nobody died." I reached under my jacket. "Here." I handed the bread to Mike, who almost dropped it. "It's potato bread."

"One bite, then pass it," Eli said.

The bread went around twice. Meanwhile, I pulled my suitcase out from under the bed and put my drawing of Irma Lee inside. I wanted to ask Mr. Hillinger about it, but I didn't want anybody else to see it.

"Where did you go?" one of the twins asked.

I told them. They didn't know about Solly, so I started with him. Then I told them about the party. "A lot of famous people were there."

"Like who?" Harvey said.

"Like Langston Hughes and W. E. B. Du Bois and a colored crook, Caspar Holstein." I couldn't remember the names of the others.

"Never heard of them," Harvey said.

"Like the prince and princess of Sheba." That shut him up. "And I got a place to stay when I leave." I told them about it.

"You'd stay with the shvartzehs?" Harvey said.

"Sure."

"How're you going to get the carving?" Mike asked.

"I've thought about that," Eli said.

We all looked at him.

"We have to spy on Mr. Doom to see if he ever leaves his office unlocked. We'll take turns."

They'd be taking a big risk to help me get out of here, to help me become an ex-buddy. Well, I might leave, but I'd be their buddy forever. "Thanks!"

Harvey said, "Good idea."

"What about Mr. Cluck?" I asked.

Jeff laughed. "Remember when Alfie and Bernie went

to the toilet at nine-thirty and didn't come back till—"

"Till after lunch," the other twin finished. "Mr. Cluck never noticed."

"Mr. Doom will kill you if he catches you," I said. I wished there was a way to take these guys with me when I left.

"Nobody's going to catch me," Harvey said. "Eli and I will go first. We'll take breakfast."

"Mr. Doom doesn't get here till after breakfast," I said. "Mr. Meltzer told me."

"Then we'll go right after breakfast."

"Where will you watch from?" I asked. "They'll notice if you look suspicious."

"I'll think of something," Harvey said.

The bell rang to wake us up. Everybody rushed back to bed before Mr. Meltzer came in. But we talked about it more on the way to breakfast. Harvey kept insisting *he* wouldn't look suspicious, but he wouldn't explain why not.

"We could stand in a stairwell, open the door a crack, and look out," I said. "Nobody in the hall would see us."

"That's a good idea," Mike said, kicking the door to the basement open, stubbing his toe, and hopping around.

"It's lousy," Harvey said. "Anybody on the stairs would see us."

"What if we just walk up and down the front halls," I said, "and act like we know where we're going."

"Boy, are you stupid," Harvey said. "Then everybody would see us."

I wanted to punch him in the nose.

"Dave's right," Eli said as we sat down at our table. "We walk along quickly like we're running an errand, and then we turn at the end of the hall and go back again if nobody's watching. If someone is watching, we go around a corner, walk along, act like we forgot something, and turn around." Eli hit his forehead with the heel of his hand, like he just remembered something. "Like that."

"But what if somebody stops us?" Mike asked.

Moe and his sidekick bullies took their places at our table.

"Then we say Mr. Cluck sent us to the library for a book." Eli ignored the bullies. "We go around the corner as if we were going to the library, and then we come back again when the coast is clear."

Harvey nodded. "That's what I'd do."

"Or, if we're going the wrong way for the library," Eli added, "we say Mr. Cluck told us to get Ed to fix something and we head for a stairwell."

"What should we do if Mr. Doom leaves?" Fred asked.

That was a dumb question. "Come and get me," I said.

"Uh-uh," Eli said. "You should only get Dave if he leaves for a special onetime reason. If it looks like he'll

do it every day, just watch to see how long he's gone."
He turned to me. "Then you'll know how much time
you have."

He was right. The food came. Moe kissed his rabbit's foot and started on my oatmeal. We stopped talking and started shoveling.

"I'll watch Mr. Doom's office first," I said when I
finished eating, "since it's my carving. You and Eli can
come after me." Just saying the words made my heart
skip. I didn't want to go near Mr. Doom's office.

Mike said he'd come with me. We were going to
do it in twos, since that's how Mr. Cluck sent us to the
toilet.

"Who'll do this afternoon?" Harvey asked. "You
know I can't do anything once Visiting Day starts."

"We only need to see if Mr. Doom locks the door
when he leaves his office before lunch," Eli said. "We'll
do it. We might be able to get in then."

Mr. Doom was all over the place while visitors were
here. He shook hands, bragged about what a fine superintendent he was, and smiled his fake smile at everybody.

Harvey yelled, "I'm not robbing anybody's office
while my mama's here."

Our bullies looked startled. "Shh," we all said.

"It's not robbery," I said. "He stole from me. And
I'm the one who's going into his office."

"Today would be the day to do it," Mike said,

knocking his spoon off the table. "He couldn't beat you too bad during Visiting Day, not with all the families here."

"He won't beat me," I said. "Because he won't catch me."

CHAPTER
27

*A*FTER BREAKFAST, MIKE and I ducked into the toilet instead of going to Mr. Cluck's classroom for Hebrew school. In the hall outside, feet thundered by.

Mike turned on all the faucets. "I hate Visiting Day."

On Visiting Day, his aunt and grandpa always came, and Mike was always extra jumpy. But he'd never said anything about it before. He turned off the faucets. "Grandpa doesn't even recognize me anymore. He took care of me till he started forgetting." He flushed the toilets. "So then I had to come here."

"He'd still take care of you if he could, wouldn't he?" Not like Ida.

"Yeah." He lifted a toilet seat and then let go of it. *Blam!*

The noise in the hall was dying down. "Shh. They'll wonder what's going on."

"Sorry."

"If nobody's in the front hall," I said, "I'm going to knock on Mr. Doom's door. I want to see if he's in there. Be ready to run."

Mike swallowed. I saw his Adam's apple bob up and down. "If he catches us, we can gang up on him."

Yeah. Mosquitoes are small, but they bite.

And one swipe kills them.

I opened the door. A prefect was at the end of the hall, walking away from us. Nobody else. We stepped out, spies entering enemy territory.

We turned into the front hall. The hall and the lobby were empty. We crossed the lobby. My hands were icy. We stood in front of Mr. Doom's office. I knocked. He rumbled, "Come in," and we ran. The stairwell door at the end of the hall looked a million miles away.

We reached the door, and slipped in. I put my fingers over my lips for Mike to be quiet, and somehow he was.

Footsteps in the hall. I stopped breathing. They came closer. Stopped. Started again. Closer, closer. Maybe farther away. Definitely farther away. Silence.

Mike started to grin. I shook my head. He might still be out there. We waited. Mike wiggled his fingers in the air, action without noise. We waited.

Mike snapped his fingers, then remembered and

stopped. Mr. Doom had to be gone by now. I started to inch the door open. I heard footsteps again. I froze. Mike froze, sort of.

The footsteps came closer. The door was open a sliver. I couldn't close it without making noise. The footsteps got louder.

I could see most of the front hall through the sliver. Mr. Doom's back came into view, walking away from us. He opened his door without using a key and went in. For all the good it did, the door had been unlocked the whole time he was in the hall.

Nothing happened after that. Mr. Doom stayed in his office. When Eli and Harvey came to take our place, we went to Mr. Cluck's class. The chart with the Hebrew alphabet was on a stand at the front of the room, but Mr. Cluck was giving his usual lecture.

As soon as I sat down my eyes closed, and I slept till the bell rang. At lunch, the twins said they'd seen Mr. Doom come out of his office and lock it right before lunch. They couldn't stop talking about their adventure.

"He locked his door. Then he walked right by us," Jeff said.

"We just rushed by like—"

"Like we were taking a message to President Coolidge."

"It was easy."

"He didn't even look at us."

I'd never get the carving if his office was always

locked when he wasn't in it.

"You can't tell anything from a weekend, Dave," Eli said, seeing my face. "He could leave his door unlocked for hours on a weekday."

"We'll find out tomorrow," Mike said.

Visiting Day lunch was the best meal of the week. This Sunday, we had stew with actual pieces of meat in it, and they weren't all gristle either. There were big chunks of potato and carrots too. Even with Moe taking his half, I felt like I had eaten.

After lunch, almost everybody went to the lobby to wait for their visitors. I went to our room along with Eli and a handful of other elevens who didn't expect anybody. As we climbed the extra flight, we heard the kids downstairs, laughing and yelling.

We were supposed to spend the time writing letters. If we didn't have any family to write to, we were supposed to study. I never wanted to study, so I always wrote a letter. If Mr. Meltzer came around that's what he saw—me writing a letter. Sometimes I wrote to Ida. Sometimes I wrote to Gideon. If I needed to figure something out, I wrote to Papa. When Visiting Day ended, I flushed the letters to Gideon and Ida, but I saved the ones to Papa.

This time my letter was to Gideon. "We just came back from lunch," I wrote.

The first course was chicken soup. When I was done I found the wishbone in the bottom of the bowl. My problem was I had nothing to wish for, it's so nice here.

After the soup they brought out stew with big pieces of meat and potatoes, and there was as much bread as we wanted to soak up the gravy. For dessert we had chocolate cookies. No one is skinny at the HHB (Heavenly Hotel for Boys).

I don't remember if I ever told you about our library. It has thousands of books, and every day we have a choice of an hour playing stickball or an hour in the library. I hit two homers yesterday.

I looked up. A few boys came in with their families. The best real thing about the HHB—the buddies—wouldn't interest Gideon.

The twins came in with an old lady who walked with a cane. Joey, who sat catty-cornered behind me in Mr. Cluck's class, was with a man who had a bushy beard. Mike must have gone somewhere else with his aunt and grandpa. Harvey didn't come in either. I had never seen his mother, and I was curious about her.

"Yesterday Mr. Gluck, our teacher, started teaching us about labor unions," I wrote.

(Remember Mr. Gluck? In my last letter I told you he's the best teacher in the whole orphanage.) Lots of kids asked questions, and Mr. Gluck answered all of them. I guess it was interesting. I didn't listen much because I was thinking about stickball.

*It would be exactly right for you here. Maybe
you'll get lucky and Uncle Jack will die and you'll be
able to*

". . . Such a good boy. Dave is smart . . ." It was Mr.
Meltzer's voice, but I didn't know what Dave he was
talking about.

I looked up. Solly, carrying a big brown paper bag
and looking as rumpled as ever, puffed along behind
Mr. Meltzer.

CHAPTER 28

"DAVE, WHY WEREN'T you downstairs waiting for your grandpa?" Mr. Meltzer sounded sickeningly friendly.

"It's about time I came, isn't it, boychik?" While Mr. Meltzer watched with a dopey grin, Solly put the bag down on my bed and held out his arms for a hug.

"Grandpa!"

Solly hugged me while thumping me on the back. It gave a rhythm to the hug. He smelled of soap and onions.

"So this is what an HHB looks like in the daytime." He turned to Mr. Meltzer. "Tell me, mister, why is it always so cold in here? Icicles are forming on my nose."

Mr. Meltzer looked embarrassed. "Uh . . . The furnace is old, and Mr. Bloom, the superintendent, believes the cold toughens the boys. You'll have to take it up

with him. Excuse me, I have to go. It's always a pleasure to see you, Mr. Gruber."

"Go, go. I didn't come to see you."

Mr. Meltzer smiled at us and left.

"Did you shmeer him again?" I asked.

"Not this time. But he wants to stay on my good
side."

"Where's Bandit?"

"He's home. I gave him the afternoon off." Solly
opened the bag and took a smaller bag out of it. "I
can't stay long. The alrightniks are expecting me."
He opened the bag and peeked inside. "I never bring
Bandit to their house. They say he's dirty." He held out
the bag. "Do you like pistachios?"

I took one (just to see if they were any good). The
elevens started to gather. They must have guessed who
Solly was. He held the bag out to Eli.

"No thank you."

Solly reached into the big bag again. "You like
peanuts?"

"We save everything for tonight," Eli said. "Put it
in your suitcase, buddy. You don't want Mr. Doo—
Bloom to catch you with food."

Solly slipped the small bag back into the big one
and gave it to me. It was nice and heavy. I put it in the
suitcase.

He pulled out his cards. "Daveleh, you want to tell
your friends' fortunes for them?"

I shuffled the cards. "Tell for you your fortune?

A quarter a card . . ." I heard gasps. "Free for buddies. Learn what the future holds. Who wants his fortune told?"

I looked around. Eli was smiling, but most of them looked serious. A lot of boys raised their hands. I picked Danny, who sat in front of me in Mr. Cluck's class.

"A wise choice," Solly said. "I can tell from the shape of your face that you have an interesting future."

"Who'll cut the cards?" I said. "Ah, Eli. Good."

Eli knocked on the cards with his knuckles, meaning they didn't need to be cut.

"Thank you." I turned a card over on my bed. The two of clubs. I whistled.

"Mazel," Solly said.

"Clubs are lucky. You will only stay at the HHB for another two years." I turned over another card. The nine of diamonds.

Solly gasped loudly.

"Diamonds stand for, uh, riches." I wished I knew more about Danny. "In two years, your long-lost uncle . . ." I turned over a card. "Your long-lost Uncle Max, who's a jack of all—"

"I don't have any uncles."

No uncles.

Solly moaned. If he was trying to help, he wasn't.

"Uh, he isn't really your uncle. He's a friend of your family, you call him 'uncle.' He will die and leave you nine thousand dollars."

By now Danny was grinning, and so were the rest of my buddies.

I turned over another card. The eight of hearts. "You will leave New York by boat and travel to eight countries."

Then, out of nowhere, I had an idea about how to gonif Moe and stop him and the other bullies from stealing our food. I'd tell everybody about it after Visiting Day was over. What a terrific idea!

"Uh," I went on, "you will stay in the eighth country, uh, Sheba . . ." I turned over another card. "Where you will marry the princess and have five children. That is your fortune. The cards have spoken. Does anybody else want his fortune told?"

I told three more fortunes—Bernie's, Louis's, and Reuben's—and then Mr. Doom walked in.

"How are my good boys?" he boomed.

I slipped the cards into Solly's pocket. I didn't know Mr. Doom's opinion about card playing, and I didn't want to find out.

We all chimed, "Fine, sir." "Good, sir." "Very good, sir." "Excellent, sir."

Joey's father or uncle or whoever he was said, "Mr. Bloom, I can't thank you enough for taking Joey." He held his hat in his hands and kept turning the brim. I thought he was going to cry. "I don't know what would have happened to him without the asylum."

"That's what we're here for, to give these boys a happy home. Am I right, boys?"

"Yes, sir."

Joey's face was bright red.

Solly frowned. Don't let him say anything, I prayed. Don't let him be a gonif with Mr. Doom.

The old lady with the twins said, "Excuse me, excuse me." She waved her cane at Mr. Doom.

Fred said in a low voice, which I could hear because of the silence, "It's all right, Grandma. We get plenty to eat."

She ignored them. "Mister, Jeffrey and Frederick are skin and bones. Are you feeding these boys? They're so—"

"What did you have for lunch today, boys?"

"Stew, sir," Jeff and Fred chanted.

"And what was in the stew?"

"Meat, sir."

"And potatoes, sir."

"Did you have enough to eat?"

"Yes, sir."

"Madam, these are active boys. We have a superlative program of physical exercise here at the HHB. Our boys get healthy food and lots of it. I was active too as a boy, and I couldn't keep flesh on my bones either." He rumbled. I think he was chuckling. "And see how big and strong I am now." The rumble stopped. "But I'll tell you what. These youngsters will share my dinner tonight. How does that sound, madam?"

The twins' grandma smelled a rat. "You don't have to do that, mister. All they need is enough to eat."

"And tonight I'll make sure they get it. Good afternoon, madam." He left.

Poor Jeff and Fred!

"So, boychik, your superintendent is a paskudnyak, a nogoodnik."

I nodded. I liked the word. "A real pass . . . pass-goo—"

"Paskudnyak."

"Paskudnyak."

"I have to go, Daveleh. I'll tell Bandit you're in good health." He patted me on the head and left.

I went back to my letter. *Every Sunday there's a chess tournament.* I stopped writing.

It was crazy. Mr. Doom was supposed to take care of all of us. Mr. Meltzer was supposed to take care of the elevens, and Mr. Cluck was supposed to teach us. None of them did what he was supposed to. When Papa died, Ida was supposed to take care of me. Or one of the relatives should have. But Solly wasn't supposed to do anything. When he saw me grab that dollar outside the rent party he could have ignored me and gone inside. Or he could have taken the money for himself. But he'd taken care of me instead—in a gonif kind of way. He'd even spent a lot of money on me. It was crazy.

"This is your lucky day, Dave." It was Mr. Meltzer again. I looked up and there were Aunt Lily and Aunt Sarah. "First your—"

"Aunt Sarah! Aunt Lily!" I yelled, so they wouldn't

hear him say "grandpa." Nobody comes for weeks, and now I'm up to my eyeballs in real relatives and fake ones.

They looked surprised that I was so glad to see them. They hugged me.

"Let me look at you," Aunt Lily said. She was carrying a brown paper bag, not as big as Solly's. "You look healthy." She saw Mr. Meltzer standing nearby, smiling goofily. "What are you waiting for?"

He stopped smiling. "Nothing." He left.

"He was hoping you'd give him money," I said.

"He should be ashamed," Aunt Sarah said, "taking money from poor people."

"We would have come sooner," Aunt Lily said, "but we've been busy. Fanny is worse."

Aunt Fanny had bad arthritis. "That's okay," I said. "I wasn't expecting anybody."

Aunt Sarah turned a little red. "I don't know how many times I thought about you. I'm always saying, 'Lily, how do you think Dave is?' Aren't I, Lily?"

She nodded. "We got three nice long letters from Gideon."

Gideon the Good.

"He says you don't write to him," Sarah said. "You should write to your brother. He worries about you. He loves you."

Aunt Lily looked around. "Nice room. So big. Nice big windows. I wish we had windows like this, don't you, Sarah?"

Aunt Sarah nodded. "It's like a palace." She rubbed her hands together for warmth. "And it's not over-heated. That's good. You can get pneumonia living in an overheated place."

"I bet you get meat every day," Aunt Lily said.

I shrugged. Meat gristle every day.

Aunt Lily went on. "And—"

Aunt Sarah interrupted. "And you never have to stand on line to go to the toilet. And there must be indoor showers with hot . . ."

They went on praising the HHB, convincing themselves it was a swell place. I thought of telling them about Mr. Doom and Papa's carving and the food stealing and Mr. Cluck. But I didn't. I didn't need Aunt Sarah and Aunt Lily when I had Irma Lee's basement.

"Here, Dave." Aunt Lily held the bag out to me.

I peeked inside. Two apples and a dozen or so of Aunt Sarah's butter cookies. My mouth watered, but I didn't eat anything. "Thanks. I'll put it away. We all share tonight." I opened my suitcase just enough to get the bag in so they wouldn't see Solly's bag. "Thanks for coming." I sounded like Gideon.

"You sound so grown up," Aunt Lily said.

"I sent a letter to your Uncle Jack," Aunt Sarah said. "I told him he should take you. I told him it was terrible to break up a family. But now that I see how nice it is here . . ."

"What do you do all day?" Aunt Lily asked.

I left out the bad stuff, so there wasn't much to say.

Then I thought of Mr. Hillinger, and I told them about him and the gesture drawing lesson. They laughed at the idea of his sister standing on a desk to pose.

They told me that Cousin Melvin had found a job as a clerk, and Ida was sewing in a dress factory and boarding with a family on Rivington Street. Then they ran out of things to say too.

We looked at each other for a few seconds. Then I said, "Thanks again for the food." And Aunt Lily said they had to leave. "We have to cook supper." They hugged me again.

"Be good," Aunt Sarah said. "Don't get in trouble."

Right.

CHAPTER
29

At FOUR-THIRTY the bell rang and the visitors left. As soon as their grandma was gone, the twins rushed to me for advice about their dinner with Mr. Doom.

"Don't do anything to make him mad," I said. "If he tells nasty lies about your family, don't argue." Then I told them to go for his spectacles if he started beating them. "But remember, he has a spare pair in his desk."

When the bell rang for dinner, Mr. Meltzer told the twins to come with him. They each ran. But Mr. Meltzer's arms snaked out. He got Jeff by the arm and Fred by his shirt collar.

We had extra recess time after dinner on Sundays. Mike and I played hit-the-penny in the courtyard. The rules are, you put a penny on the ground and each person walks an equal distance away from it. Then you try to hit the penny with a ball, and you keep track. Whoever gets to twenty-one first wins and keeps the penny.

After I beat Mike twice, we played tag with our buddies. It was fun, but I kept worrying about Fred and Jeff, and I finally left the game. The twins weren't in our room, but Eli and Harvey were there. Eli was reading, and Harvey was looking out the window.

"Did the twins come back?" I asked.

Eli shook his head. Harvey didn't say anything.

"I'm going to the nurse," I said. "They might be there."

Eli came with me.

"How long have you lived here?" I asked him in the hall.

"I came when I was seven."

"Did you ever try to run away?"

"Uh-uh." He pointed at his teeth, with the wires on them. "They're straightening my teeth."

"You're staying for your teeth?"

"Not only that. In the summer they send us to camp, which is fun. Much better than here. And Mr. Cluck is the only bad teacher I've had. Last year we had Mr. Silver, and he was really good."

I didn't care about teachers except for Mr. Hillinger. Upstairs, the door to the infirmary was shut. When we got close, I heard a man's voice, not Mr. Doom's rumble.

I knocked. A nurse opened the door—not my nurse, a stranger.

I glimpsed a doctor's bag, part of a man's back bent over someone on the cot. And Jeff, sitting on a chair, looking pale, but healthy.

"Can you tell us how the twins are?" Eli asked, sounding just right for talking to a grown-up.

"They'll live." She slammed the door.

Inside, one of them screamed.

When Eli and I got back to our room, Harvey was still at the window. "How're the twins?" he asked.

The bell rang. Recess was over.

Eli shrugged. "Jeff looked all right. We saw him for a second. The doctor was there."

The other elevens started coming in. Mr. Meltzer sat down at his table. I went to him. He'd brought in a new photograph of his wife and daughters. What kind of papa could he be?

"What happened to Fred and Jeff?" I asked.

He didn't answer right away, but he finally said, "Jeff is fine. Fred fell and broke his arm."

Fell-shmell! Mr. Doom broke Fred's arm. It would be a twig in Mr. Doom's big, meaty hands.

After the lights went out we always waited before sharing the treats. We wanted the prefect on guard duty to think we were asleep. About five minutes after lights-out I had to go to the toilet. And that's when I made my lovely discovery. There was no prefect in the hall.

When I got back to our room I told everybody. They got out of bed immediately.

"Congratulations," Eli said. "They've stopped worrying about you. It's Mr. Drucker's turn tonight. He must be playing poker right this minute."

"I bet Mr. Meltzer told them about the shmeer," Mike said, bouncing on his bed. "They want to stay on your good side, Dave."

This was wonderful. I'd be able to sneak out once I got the carving.

We piled our treats on Mr. Meltzer's table. Eli sat in the chair, while the rest of us stood in the narrow aisles or sat on the nearest beds. I stood near Eli, and Mike stood next to me.

Eli held up a salami. "Harvey, buddy," he said, "I need your knife."

"Good thing I have it." I saw a glint of silver.

Eli sliced off a chunk of salami. "For Fred and Jeff." He put the chunk down on Mr. Meltzer's table. Then he cut a slice. "Take one thin slice." He passed the salami and knife to Danny.

I peeled off my slice when it was my turn. Salami has so much flavor. I sucked on my piece instead of chewing it.

For once I had goodies to share. Out of Solly's brown bag came raisins, sucking candy, a big soft pretzel with lots of salt, and a banana. Plus the nuts. Plus the cookies and the two apples from Aunt Sarah and Aunt Lily.

"Whole orphans don't always have it so bad," I said.

"Yeah," Harvey said. "If you're a whole, at least you know where your mama is."

I should have known his mother hadn't come, because he'd skipped recess.

After the food was gone, we wandered away to our beds. As I drifted off to sleep, I remembered my idea for stopping the bullies from stealing our food, and then I was out, asleep.

I heard a noise, and half woke up, but I rolled over and fell back to sleep.

And then—it could have been an hour later or a minute—somebody hissed, "Psst, Dave. Wake up."

I sat up, wide awake, scared.

It was Jeff. "Here." He held something up. "It was in Mr. Doom's desk."

I reached out, and Jeff put a key into my hand.

CHAPTER
30

THE KEY WAS on a ring along with a flat metal disk.
"How's Fred?" I whispered.

"He broke his arm. They took him to the hospital to put a cast on it."

"How's Fred?" Eli asked, coming toward us. Everyone was waking up and crowding around my bed.

"He broke his arm," Jeff said.

I wondered if he broke it getting the key. "What happened?"

"Mr. Doom lied about sharing his dinner. There was no food. When we got to his office he started talking. At first he didn't make any sense. He said something about, uh, 'culture' and his wife liking to read about high society. Then—"

"He talked that way to me too," I said. I guess he started every beating the same way.

"Then he said how much it costs to feed us. We remembered what you said and we didn't argue." Jeff sat on the edge of my bed. "But he got madder and madder anyway. He kept talking softly, but you could tell." Jeff stopped.

"How?" Mike asked.

"He started smacking his yardstick into the palm of his hand."

"Oy vay," Joey said.

Jeff went on. "He said it was easy for lazy yentas like our grandma to complain. Smack, smack with the yardstick." Jeff turned to me. "I was thinking about running when Fred raced for the door."

"Then what?" Harvey said.

"Mr. Doom is fast. Fred wouldn't have gotten out of the office if I hadn't yelled, 'Bully! Pig! Stinker!'"

Even in the dark, I saw that Jeff was grinning. And I heard it in his voice.

"It was the best I could think of. Anyway, Mr. Doom turned, and Fred got out, and Mr. Doom went after him. That's when I thought of your carving, buddy."

Buddy. He sure was.

"I went to the knickknack cabinet but it was locked, like you said. So I ran to his desk, and a key was there, right in front. I started towards the cabinet to see if the key opened it, but then Fred hollered, and I ran out to help him. Sorry."

"That's okay. Thanks, buddy." I shook his hand.

"Then what happened?" Eli asked.

"Joey's papa came in."

"My papa?"

"Yeah. Fred was running up the stairs to the balcony. I didn't see this part. He told me about it. He said he wasn't thinking straight or he would have stayed by the wall, not the banister, because all Mr. Doom had to do was reach through and grab him. Fred pulled away hard and he fell. He put out his hand to catch himself, and that's how he broke his arm."

"What did my papa do?"

Jeff didn't answer for a few seconds, and I realized he was crying. "Mr. Doom didn't care that Fred was screaming. He stood over him, hitting him with the yardstick and yelling, 'Teach you . . . Teach you . . .' And then your papa came in." Jeff choked out a laugh. "The second the door started to open, Mr. Doom was hugging Fred and asking him if he was hurt and telling him to be brave."

"What was Papa doing here?"

"He forgot his hat."

"Where was Mr. Meltzer?" I asked.

"I didn't see him when I ran out of the office, but he was there a minute or so after Joey's father came. He took us to the infirmary and then he left."

We were quiet for a minute, thinking about Mr. Doom.

"He shouldn't be in charge of a zoo," Danny said, "much less us."

"Here," Eli said. He handed Jeff his share of the

Visiting Day treats. "You didn't get any dinner."

"We should tell the police," Mike said.

"Who'd believe a bunch of halfs and wholes?" Harvey said.

"I hate him," Mike said. "I'd like to punch him. I'd like to punch his nose in."

I sat down next to Jeff.

"We have a roof over us," Eli said. "We aren't starving. It could be worse."

"Our families feel better because we're here," Joey said.

Yeah. Ida felt a lot better. I stretched out and got under my blanket. Jeff started to get up, but I told him he could stay.

"I wish he could be one of us for a day," Harvey said, "and see what it's like."

"If he was one of us," Jeff said while chewing, "Fred and I would beat the living daylights out of him. We'd break *both* his arms."

I closed my eyes. I pushed the key under my pillow and covered it with my hand. Around me everybody was still talking. It was nice, aside from the topic. Cozy. I was going to miss them.

Later, I woke up because I needed to use the toilet again. I took the key with me. The chair at the end of the hall was still empty. I wondered where the prefects had their poker game.

In the hall light I looked at the key, which was small and made of brass. The metal disk on the key ring had

writing on it. "To Mordecai Bloom," it said. "A beneficent leader of boys and men." I didn't know what
beneficent meant, but unless it meant lousy, rotten, and
paskudnyak, it was way off base. The other side said,
"HHB Board of Directors."

Back in our room, I fell asleep holding the key.
When the wake-up bell rang, my hand was cramped
and the key was still in it.

After I got dressed, I put the key in one pocket and
the drawing of Irma Lee folded up small in the other.
I wanted to show the drawing to Mr. Hillinger so he
could tell me how to do faces better.

Fred came in with his arm in a cast. Everybody went
to him, wanting to know how he was. He said he was
okay and wiggled his fingers at the end of the cast.
He started to tell us what had happened, and he was
annoyed that Jeff had beaten him to it.

I walked to breakfast with the twins, Mike, Harvey,
and Eli. "At breakfast," I said, "call me 'wizard' and act
scared of me." I wanted to try out my idea to stop the
food stealing.

"Why should I?" Harvey said.

"Dave has a good reason," Mike said, scratching
his ear. "He has something up his sleeve."

"Okay, Harvey," I said. "Call Eli 'wizard,' and act
scared of him. I will too." That would be better, since I
was leaving, and the wizard had to be here if this was
going to work. Eli would make a fine gonif. He'd fool
Moe because he always seemed so serious and honest.

"Just make sure the bullies notice, especially Moe." I told them my idea. They all liked it, even Harvey. Breakfast would set the stage. We'd get ready during morning recess, and at lunch we'd do it.

In the dining hall, I sat next to Eli, and a minute later Moe squeezed between us. When he kissed his rabbit's foot, I stuck my head around him and yelled, "Wizard, does that really do any good?"

Eli shook his head. "If it was a black rabbit, he'd have something. But a white rabbit's foot only carries germs."

"Huh? How does he know?" Moe asked.

"He knows," I said.

From across the table, Fred waved his cast. "See this?"

The ladies started carrying the coffins out of the kitchen. Everybody knew about Fred's broken arm. Everybody always knew when Mr. Doom beat somebody.

Jeff held his unbroken arms up. "And see this? Not a scratch."

"So what?" asked Moe.

"He cast a spell to protect me," Jeff said.

"I didn't have time to do Fred," Eli said.

The coffin reached us. Moe started on my food while keeping an eye on Eli. When Eli reached Moe's way for the water pitcher, Moe drew back a little.

Good. I might be able to do something for my buddies before I left.

CHAPTER
31

W HEN WE GOT to our classroom after breakfast, Mr. Hillinger was putting a flute on Mr. Cluck's desk. I wondered what it was for.

Stacks of notebook-size paper were on our desks. When we sat down, Mr. Hillinger walked around giving us boxes of colored chalk from a big paper bag. "Good morn . . . You'll have to share the pastels, I'm afr . . . Although it's not so . . . A limited palette is good. Good disci . . ."

There were eight sticks of chalk in the box Mike and I were supposed to share. The red chalk was in two pieces, and the blue was a half-inch nubbin.

"Today we're going to draw to express . . . to show feeling or a mood. An artist can say he's angry or . . . You only *think* you need words . . . It could be any feeling." He played three long slow notes on the flute.

"How does that make you feel, boys?"

Nobody said anything. I raised my hand. "Sad?"

"Good, Dave. Anybody feel anything else?"

Harvey raised his hand. "Definitely lazy."

"Good too. Other boys may feel something else. I'll play . . . Remember what we've learned . . . Draw over the whole page. Composition is . . . Listen." He played more sad music.

I stared at my stack of paper. I didn't know how to draw sadness. A face crying? How did you draw tears? Mike had gone to work already, but he was drawing violins.

And then I knew what to do. I held the purple chalk on its side and covered the page with purple. Mike had the black. I borrowed it and broke it in half. Now we both had black.

From the right side of the page I drew part of a long rectangle. The rest of it you had to imagine, because it was off the page. I filled the rectangle in so it was solid black. To the left of it I drew a man bent over from carrying his end of the box. You saw him from the side, and I filled him in in black too. Behind him came a woman. One of her feet was in the air, so you could tell she was walking. She was following the man.

The room was quiet. When had Mr. Hillinger stopped playing? He started a happy song, but I kept drawing the sad one. I drew a boy following the woman. I swallowed around the lump in my throat. Another man came after the boy. None of them touched each other. That was important.

Mr. Hillinger walked through the aisles while he played. He walked by me drawing the first song. I kept going, rushing to catch up with everybody.

I finished. Seven and a quarter people followed the coffin. You only saw a hand and a leg of the eighth person all the way on the left side of the page. The people weren't much more than stick figures. But the picture was sad. I had never seen such a sad picture. I had done it, drawn sadness. It felt grand. Sad, but grand.

I took a new sheet of paper and tried to think what a happy drawing would be, but Mr. Hillinger stopped playing. "Here's another . . ." He looked at his watch. "We have time for . . . Take a new sheet, Eli. No more music. Here's a poem to . . . Draw whatever it makes you . . ." He recited:

> " 'Twas brillig, and the slithy toves
> Did gyre and gimble in the wabe:
> All mimsy were the borogroves,
> And the mome raths outgrabe."

He went on. How were we supposed to draw that? It didn't mean anything. Some of the words meant something, and for a second I thought I understood, but then it was gone. There was a son and some monsters, a "Jubjub bird" and a "frumious Bandersnatch," which sounded like an animal to sic on Mr. Doom.

I drew a green lion with big twisty horns coming out of its mane, a red rabbit that was bigger than the lion, and a yellow goat upside down and high on the page. Around the animals I drew shapes that fitted into each other.

Mr. Hillinger came down our aisle. At my desk he picked up my funeral picture and stared at it for a long time. When he put it down again he said, "Very nice, Dave. Fine."

"Mr. Hillinger . . ." I took the drawing of Irma Lee out of my pocket and unfolded it. "I messed up her face. How do you draw faces?" I hated showing it to him. I hated to look at it, with the stupid one eye in the wrong place.

He studied the drawing. "You like to draw?"

"Yeah. Yes, sir. I do."

He raised his voice for everyone to hear. "Listen, boys. You draw faces just like everything . . . They're no different. We shouldn't be frightened by a nose or a mouth . . . Be sure to bring your faces on Friday. You're going to do por . . ." He handed the messed-up picture back to me without saying anything else. He probably didn't want to hurt my feelings by talking about it. "Now hold up the drawing you like best," he told the class. "You should see what your . . . Look at what ideas you all . . ."

I held up the funeral picture. Everybody else held up their happy drawings. Joey's was of food—a cake, an ice-cream cone, and something that might have been a chicken. Eli had drawn a lake with a sailboat. Mike's was pink, blue, and orange guess-whats. I liked Harvey's, which was a smile that filled the whole page. I didn't tell him, though.

He had something to say about mine, of course. "You shouldn't have colored the background purple. There should be trees or houses."

"That smile you drew is too big," Mike said, sticking up for me. "And it's too—"

Mr. Cluck came in.

"Boys," Mr. Hillinger said, "show Mr. Gluck your . . . Aren't they hand . . . You must be so proud to . . ."

Mr. Cluck bustled to the front of the room. Ira and Joey raised their hands to go to the toilet. It was their turn to watch Mr. Doom's office. I'd forgotten all about it.

Mr. Hillinger started collecting our blank paper and chalk. "Save your drawings, boys. You can . . . Mr. Gluck, may I borrow Dave for a . . . He can help me . . ." He gestured, and I knew he wanted me to help him get the chalk and the paper.

Mr. Cluck said, "All right, if he is any help."

Mr. Hillinger had gotten almost everything already, but I walked along the desks by the window and picked up the rest.

"Now if you'll . . ."

I put the chalk and paper into the paper bag. Mr. Hillinger picked up the bag. "Would you be so . . ."

I took the flute and followed him into the hall and

out to the lobby, where Ira and Joey were walking quickly, looking like they were on an important errand—except when they saw Mr. Hillinger, who knew they were supposed to be going to the toilet. Ira stopped. Joey slowed down, then grabbed Ira's arm and tugged him along.

"Hello, boys." Mr. Hillinger smiled at them and kept going till we reached the front door.

"Dave, would you . . . On Thursdays . . . It would mean missing school, just an afternoon. Everyone is talented, but . . ."

I wouldn't mind missing the whole week, but what did he mean?

"A few . . . Such ability . . . I teach a few boys . . . It's a special . . ."

I started nodding. If he was saying he had a special drawing class, I wanted to be in it. "Yes," I said. "For drawing? I'd like to . . ." I sounded as jumbled as he did.

He smiled broadly. "Wonderf . . . It's not just . . . We paint too. Oils, watercol . . . You're very . . ." He took the flute from me. "I'm so glad. You have . . ." He opened the HHB door.

Finish the sentence, I thought. Finish it! What do I have?

". . . a gift." He left.

CHAPTER 32

a GIFT! I didn't just like to draw, I didn't just have the beginnings of an eye, I had a gift!

I watched him go down the path to the gate. He had a funny walk. His right shoulder was higher than his left, possibly because of all the stuff he was carrying. I tried to memorize the way he looked from behind. When I got back to our classroom I wanted to draw it.

I couldn't wait for Thursday. I couldn't wait for every Thursday!

Wait for every Thursday! But I wouldn't be here every Thursday, not after I got the carving back. I'd miss out on the special class.

I stopped walking. Didn't I want to get out of here as soon as I could? Sure I did. But I also wanted to be in that class. And I wanted to go on being with my buddies. But I'd sworn to get the carving and leave. I couldn't do both, stay and leave. I hated it here. Well, I hated the HHB. My buddies and Mr. Hillinger weren't the HHB, and I didn't hate them. I liked them—a lot, a whole lot.

I started walking again. I had to figure it out.

Back in class, Mike was drawing violins. Mr. Cluck was babbling. I tried to draw Mr. Hillinger walking away from me. You'd think it would be easy to show he was going the other way, but it kept looking like he was coming toward me. You'd think I could get it right, since I had a gift.

The bell rang for morning recess. Time to get ready for Moe.

In the courtyard, Eli explained my idea to all the elevens. Harvey said he'd thought it over and it would never work. Nobody listened to him, and we started rehearsing, all of us except Danny and Louis, who would be watching Mr. Doom's office during lunch. I concentrated on the rehearsal, but every so often I'd remember what Mr. Hillinger had said, about my having a gift.

And then I'd see us elevens in my mind, the way we were standing right now, the expressions on our faces. And I'd imagine a drawing, a gesture drawing of all of us.

Then I'd be back in the middle of the rehearsal again.

There were a few tricky moments in the plan, and it might not work, and it might get Moe mad at us, which would make everything worse. But if it succeeded we'd get to eat our entire lousy meals from now on.

"What about the eights and the nines and the tens?" Mike asked. "Can't we help them?"

"They'll have to think of their own nutty plan," Harvey said.

I usually sat next to Mike at lunch, but today Eli was on my right and Mike was across the table next to Jeff. I didn't want Mike too near me, because Moe was going to pick on somebody, and I didn't want it to be him.

Eli and I sat close together, hoping our bullies would sit on the other side of each of us. If one of them sat between us, we'd have to wait till supper to try again.

Moe came in and sat on my left, and Eli's bully sat on Eli's right. So far so good. Moe kissed his rabbit's foot and picked up his fork. A lady began dishing out the food at our table. She served Moe. He took a bite. She served me. His fork headed my way.

"Wait!"

He hesitated for a second. It was enough. I passed my plate to Eli. Eli's bully was eating Eli's food. All the elevens were watching Eli and Moe and me, but they were eating at the same time.

Eli spread his hands over my plate and started humming. I don't know how he did it, but the hum had an echo. It sounded round and full. He closed his eyes and swayed. The hum rose and fell.

He wasn't a bad gonif. He was doing fine.

He stopped humming and nodded his head three times. "Thank you, oh Phantoms of the Just." When he said *phantoms* he hummed the *m* so it sounded like *phantom-m-ms*. He returned the plate to me.

"Now you can eat it," I told Moe. I folded my hands in my lap. "It's all yours."

Moe stuck his fork in, lifted it.

I held my breath. It was all over if he ate.

He stopped an inch from his lips. "What's wrong with it?"

"The wizard said I shouldn't eat it. He said it's for you."

Moe put his fork down and reached around me and grabbed Eli's shoulder. "Wha—"

Eli didn't even look scared. He waved a hand in front of Moe and started humming again.

Moe let go. "Stop that."

Eli kept humming.

Mike's bully reached across the table and started to take my food.

Moe grabbed the edge of the plate. "Watch yourself."

The other bully let go. "I thought you didn't want it."

"You thought wrong." Moe looked over at Eli, who had stopped humming and was sitting with his head down, swaying. Moe looked around at all of us elevens. Mike moved and caught Moe's eye. "You. I mean you." He pushed my plate toward Mike and lifted the fork loaded with my food. "Hungry?"

We were in trouble.

Mike shook his head. "No, thank you."

"Eat it." He handed Mike the fork.

"Don't eat it!" I yelled.

"Don't," Eli said. "The Phantom-m-ms will be angry."

"Eat." Moe stood up. "Eat."

Mike put the food in his mouth, which was what he was supposed to do if this happened. Then he was supposed to fall backwards off the bench and lie still. But when we rehearsed he couldn't lie still. Nobody in a million years would have believed he had fainted.

Mike chewed once and swallowed. He started to smile, but the smile froze and he pointed wildly at his throat. His eyeballs rolled back so only the whites showed. Then he fell backwards, but he didn't lie still. His hands clawed the air. He rolled from side to side. He made choking noises.

He was the best gonif of us all.

I looked at Moe. He was clutching his rabbit's foot with both hands. Boys from nearby tables were gathering around Mike. Then I saw Mike's bully laugh, not believing any of it. His fork was heading for my plate. If he ate, Moe would know we had tricked him and he'd murder us.

Jeff also must have seen the bully go for my plate. He leaned on the table as if to see Mike better. When he put his hand on the table, he knocked his water glass into my plate, sending them both flying. The glass broke, and the food slid all over the floor. And Mike's bully looked very disappointed.

Mr. Meltzer pushed through the ring of boys around Mike. He picked Mike up and carried him to the nearest stairway, probably on the way to the infirmary. I wondered what Mike would do when the nurse examined him.

A serving lady started cleaning up the broken glass and spilled food. Moe leaned away from Eli. With both hands, Eli traced Moe's outline in the air. He started humming again.

"Don't!" Moe yelled. "Stop!"

Eli went on shaping the air around Moe. His humming got louder and deeper.

"Stop it!"

"Hum-m-m-m. He will change his ways." He put a hum into the *n* too so it sounded like *chan-n-nge*. "He will chan-n-nge, or bad luck will follow him-m-m everywhere. Hum-m-m. Nothing will go right for him-m-m ever again-n-n. Now will he obey me?"

"What? How?"

"Feed me!"

Moe looked confused. We had all finished eating. "There's no food."

"You have taken-n-n the food of others. The Phan-n-ntom-m-ms are an-n-ngry."

"I didn't! You saw! I didn't eat it."

"Before this meal. The Phan-n-ntom-m-ms wan-n-nt reven-n-nge."

"No, they don't. They couldn't!" Moe's voice cracked. "I'm sorry. I didn't know."

"These are the Phan-n-ntom-m-ms' wishes." Eli paused.

"What? What wishes?"

"You will take no more food from-m-m an-n-ny eleven-n-n. When-n-n we are twelve you still will take no food from-m-m us. You will forbid an-n-nyon-n-ne to take food from-m-m us. These are the wishes of the Phan-n-ntom-m-ms. Do you hear an-n-nd will you obey?"

"Tell them not to be mad. Uh, I hear and I will obey."

It was torture not to laugh. I looked down at the floor. If I looked at any of the elevens I'd never stop laughing. If I looked at Moe I'd die from-m-m laughing.

I stared at the floor. I didn't want to leave this. I didn't want to leave my buddies.

CHAPTER
33

WHEN WE LEFT the dining room, Bernie and
Reuben went to take over Mr. Doom patrol
duty from Louis and Danny. Moe walked
with us to our classroom. It's a good thing he didn't
peek inside, because there was Mike, looking healthy
and only twitching as much as he usually did.

"Did it work?" Mike asked when I sat down.

Fred passed by, laughing. "Uh, what are your wishes,
wizard?"

"It worked," I told Mike. "You were terrific."

"Tell them-m-m not to be mad," Jeff said, following
his brother down the aisle. "Tell the phan-n-ntom-m-ms."

Mr. Cluck picked up his lecture where he had left
off before lunch. I opened my notebook and started
doodling, writing *gift* in different fancy letters. Of
course I would leave. I had sworn that I would, and

I would. When I got the carving back.

And I would get it back. Someday. It would take a while to get into Mr. Doom's office. It could take a month. Or a year. But when I did and I got my carving, then I'd say farewell to the Hell Hole for Brats.

Meanwhile, I would make the best of it. I turned the page in my notebook and started to draw Danny, who was chewing on the end of his pen and staring up at the ceiling.

The classroom door opened, and Louis, Reuben, and Bernie came in. But Reuben and Bernie were supposed to be watching Mr. Doom's office. Something had happened.

On the way to his desk, Louis stopped by me and whispered, "At lunchtime he goes out and leaves the door open so the maid can clean his office."

I could get Papa's carving. Tomorrow I'd have it. "Thanks," I whispered back. "Swell!"

It *was* swell. But the lump in my throat was bigger than ever.

I skipped going to the courtyard during evening recess. In our room I sat on my bed and opened my notebook. "Dear Papa," I wrote. "Soon I'll have your carving. I won't have to be a prisoner here anymore."

I tried to picture Papa smiling while he read the words. But he wouldn't smile. I couldn't make him. He didn't want me to live in a basement, no matter how fine the house above it was.

That got me mad. He'd left me in this mess. What right did he have to tell me where I should live? What right did he have to tell me I should stay in a place I hated?

In my imagination he laughed. "You're making trouble for yourself, rascal. You don't hate it."

"You're wrong, Papa," I wrote. "I hate being locked in. I hate freezing all the time. I hate Mr. Doom, and Mr. Cluck, and Mr. Meltzer." I stared at the words. They were true, but they weren't the whole story.

I pictured Papa's carving. And, at the end of the line, after all the animals and after Papa and Mama and Gideon and me, I pictured the elevens and Mr. Hillinger lined up, waiting their turn to board the ark.

I didn't want to leave them behind. I didn't want to sail off without them.

After lights-out I sat up in bed. "Hey, buddies," I whispered.

They started to crowd around.

"This better be good," Harvey said. "I was drifting off."

Harvey! I had forty-one reasons for staying, and he was the only one of them who annoyed me most of the time.

"Tomorrow I'll get my carving back, and I want to thank everybody for risking your—"

"We always help a buddy," Harvey whispered. "We never—"

"When are you going to run away?" Mike was scratching his side and hopping.

"That's what I was going to—"

"Don't tell us," Harvey said. "That way Mr. Doom can't torture it out of us."

"I'm trying to—"

"We need to know when," Eli said. "We may have to cover—"

I almost screamed. "I'm not leaving! For ten minutes I've been trying to tell you that—"

Mike started pumping my hand. "You're not leaving!" He slapped me on the back. "You're staying!"

"How come?" Harvey sounded suspicious.

"Um . . . It's because . . ." I swallowed. "I'll never find buddies like you anywhere. Um, there's no point trying. Uh, and I'd just miss—"

"Good," Eli said. "I hate to lose a buddy."

"You were crazy to want to live with the shvartzehs anyway," Harvey said.

"They're better than you," I said.

"Take that back!"

"I won't!"

"Cut it out," Eli said. "Somebody will hear you. You can fight tomorrow." He started laughing. "You two love each other so much you want to kill each other."

I laughed too, and Harvey joined in.

"I don't want to fight you," I added. "You just don't know anything about colored people."

"What's to know?"

Irma Lee. Jazz. Mrs. Packer. Irma Lee. Rent parties. People having fun together. Aaron Douglas. Langston Hughes. A painting of Noah's ark. Irma Lee. I didn't say anything. I just got the rope out of my suitcase and started getting dressed.

"You're going out?" Mike said.

"Yeah." I was going to meet Solly. But it was too early to leave. I sat on my bed and waited. My buddies went back to bed.

Would Irma Lee be mad when I told her I wasn't going to live in her basement? She'd been so excited about having me there. But I'd still be her friend. I'd still get out and see her.

The clock struck eleven. I stuffed my bed with my pajamas and my towel and Mike's towel, which I borrowed without waking him up to ask. Buddies could do stuff like that.

The prefects played poker in a classroom on the first floor, according to Mike. I heard them laughing and yelling as soon as I opened the door from the stairwell. They were making too much noise to hear me, but they'd catch me if one of them decided to go to the toilet. I raced to the lobby, feeling like a hunted rabbit. I made it.

For the first time, it was colder outside than in. I climbed the oak tree. When I reached the branch that hung over the street, I tied my rope to it and let the end hang down on the street side of the fence. I used it to shinny down, and then I climbed back up, just to be sure. It worked. I was out, and I could get back in.

I walked off whistling the song about Sadie Lou. Everything was going my way.

Solly wasn't at the Tree of Hope. It was the right tree, because a man with a clarinet told me it was.

"Are you a musician, sonny?" he said. "You're short on years and pigmentation to be looking here for a job."

I said I was just waiting for someone.

"That's good." He started playing softly.

I was probably early. Solly had said he'd wait for me from twelve to one, and it might not even be midnight yet. I stamped my feet to keep warm.

A man walked by, touched the tree, and kept walking. Two more people came and did the same. A gray Cadillac—a V-8—pulled up at the curb. The chauffeur got out and opened the back door, and a white woman got out.

I knew her. She was the maid who'd led us through the crowd at Irma Lee's party.

"Mr. Dave?" She came toward me.

Me?

"Mrs. Packer would like you to be her dinner guest tonight."

My mouth watered. Dinner.

And Irma Lee. "Okay."

"Come with me." She turned back to the car.

Hold on. "Can I come later? I'm supposed to meet somebody."

"Mr. Solly is waiting for you at Mrs. Packer's residence."

Then it was all right. "Can I ride in front?"

"Certainly."

The chauffeur led me around the car and opened the door for me. The seats were dark green leather, and the whole inside smelled of leather. I slid behind the wheel. The top of it was even with the bridge of my nose. If I ducked down a little I could see the road and my feet could reach the pedals. There was the key. You didn't have to crank a Cadillac. I put out my hand—and the chauffeur opened his door. I slid back.

"Nice car."

"Glad you like it." The silver buttons on his uniform clicked against the steering wheel as he got in. He turned the key and pushed a button, and the motor started. We pulled out into the street. "Do you want to steer?"

Nah. I could steer a Cadillac any old time. Sure I did! I slid close to him, but I couldn't see the road, so I got up on my knees. I leaned across him to take the wheel.

"You have to let me see too," he said, slowing down and moving me over. "There."

I held the steering wheel steady, even though it vibrated like anything. We drove slowly down the street. I wished Irma Lee lived in California.

How fast were we going? Only fifteen, but the speedometer went up to a hundred and twenty.

"Turn right at the corner." He slowed down even more.

I started turning. Not enough. The wheel wasn't easy to turn. I pulled harder, putting my whole body into it. There. No—too far. We were going to go up on the sidewalk. The chauffeur turned the wheel back, but I could have done it. We were going straight again. There was Irma Lee's house.

"Pull up here."

I turned the wheel and got it right this time. We stopped.

"Thank you," I said.

"Thank you," he said.

The house seemed strange without the crowd outside and the hundreds inside. The front room was nice, now that I could see it, with purple wallpaper and a mahogany electric fireplace.

"Follow me," the maid said. In the doorway to the dining room she stopped and announced, "Mr. Dave is here."

I went in. Irma Lee was near the end of the table. Part of her face was blocked by a silver candleholder. Mrs. Packer was next to her. Irma Lee was wearing a yellow dress, and her hair was in braids tied with yellow ribbon. Seeing her made me want to dance the Charleston.

Solly was on Mrs. Packer's left with his back to me. The parrot flapped its wings and squawked, "Mazel tov."

I smiled at Irma Lee and waved, but she looked away.

CHAPTER
34

"ᗪAVE!" MRS. PACKER stood and came toward me.
"I'm so glad you could make it." She took me
to the chair next to Solly.

A colored man I hadn't noticed came from somewhere and pulled my chair out. A butler? A real butler?

"Mama . . ." Irma Lee said.

"Yes, baby child?"

"Nothing." She looked down at her lap. She hadn't
smiled at me once.

"So, boychik. Here we are with the leisure class
again."

"We're ready for dinner now, George," Mrs. Packer
told the butler.

He disappeared into the kitchen.

Mrs. Packer turned to me. "What are you studying
in school, Dave?"

I wasn't studying anything. I was trying not to listen to Mr. Cluck's bellyaching. "Umm . . . Uh . . . Geography. We're supposed to learn the states and what their capitals are."

"Baby girl knows all that. Don't you, honey?"

Irma Lee looked at Mrs. Packer, quick and hard, and then went back to staring at her lap.

A maid came in and put a steaming bowl of soup in front of each of us. Nobody said anything. The only sounds were the click of the maid's heels and the clink when she put the soup bowl on top of our plates. I picked up my soup spoon. It weighed a pound. Real silver.

Irma Lee lifted her head and looked at me. She was almost crying. I wished I knew what was wrong.

"Do you like terrapin soup, Dave?" Mrs. Packer asked.

The parrot squawked, "Ess, kinder."

I tasted it and nodded. It was delicious, whatever it was.

"Terrapin is turtle in a tuxedo, boychik."

"Eat it while it's hot, baby girl."

Irma Lee put her spoon in the soup and stirred it a little.

The maid came back to whisk away our soup bowls.

"Did you like the band Saturday night, Solly?" Mrs. Packer asked.

"There's no jazz music I don't like."

The maid was back with plates of salad.

"Have you heard Fletcher Henderson's band yet?"

"Once. Bandit and I stomped at the Savoy."

They went on talking about jazz. The salad plates were taken away, and the main dish arrived: lamb chops, roasted potatoes, peas and carrots. I ate everything. Irma Lee ate nothing, but she moved her food around, especially when her mama looked at her.

Now they were talking about Germany joining the League of Nations. Dessert came. Apple pie with raisins in it. Coffee for Solly and Mrs. Packer.

Irma Lee looked at me and mouthed some words. I shrugged to show I didn't understand, and she tried again. At least she didn't seem mad at me, but I still didn't understand.

"We can take our coffee into the library." Mrs. Packer stood up.

Solly grunted as he stood too. "By me, that's where I always have it."

I hung back so I could walk next to Irma Lee. "Hi," I whispered.

"Sorry." She touched my arm. "I didn't mean . . ." Her eyes filled up. "I was careful."

I didn't understand. We were in the library, the room with all the books, naturally.

"The green chair is very comfortable," Mrs. Packer told Solly.

He sank into it. "Oy, I won't be able to get up."

Mrs. Packer sat on a dark red sofa. She patted the pillow next to her. "Baby girl . . ."

Irma Lee sat on a flowered chair across from Solly. She was tiny in it, and she patted the space next to herself, exactly the way her mama had. I sat in the chair with her. Our knees touched.

"Dave," Mrs. Packer said, "baby child thinks I'm being cruel, but—"

"You are! Dave needs—"

"Baby child, listen to me. Dave doesn't need—"

"Stop calling me that."

Mrs. Packer said, "I went out this afternoon to visit a friend." She turned to Solly. "I couldn't take babe—Irma Lee, because Augusta isn't well, and I didn't want babe—Irma Lee to catch a germ. More coffee?"

Solly shook his head. "No, thank you."

"But the doctor was there, so I came home. I called baby girl, but she didn't answer. So I hunted for her, and I found her in the basement."

I began to get it. Next to me, Irma Lee shifted. I turned, and she was crying.

"Honey," Mrs. Packer said to her, "you didn't do a thing wrong. You were a good and true friend. Dave, you should have seen the things baby girl had down there waiting for you. Cushions from an old sofa, five pillows at least, paper and crayons and—"

"Mama, stop!"

"Dave, I keep telling her that you'll understand. I can't have you living in my basement. I'd—"

"The boychik was going to . . ."

So that's what was wrong. That's why Irma Lee was

sorry. She thought she'd let me down. But she hadn't. She never would, not on purpose. "It's all right. I don't—"

"See? I told you. Dave doesn't mind." Mrs. Packer turned to Solly. "I had another idea. If I helped his family . . ." She stopped and looked uncomfortable, shifted on the couch. "I could perhaps help a relative. A bigger apartment . . ."

Look at this! Mrs. Packer didn't want me so bad she'd pay my relatives to take me.

"Wait." I held up my hand before she said anything else. "Irma Lee, I was going to tell you tonight that I decided to stay at the orphanage."

She flew out of our chair. Her face was streaked with tears. "I hate you, Dave Caros!" She ran out of the library.

I started to go after her, then stopped. I couldn't run all over somebody else's house.

"Go ahead," Mrs. Packer said. She chuckled. "Poor baby girl doesn't . . ."

I didn't hear the rest. I pounded up the stairs and knocked on the door to Irma Lee's room. She didn't say anything, but I went in anyway. She was sprawled across her bed. She didn't make a sound.

Her bedspread was all rumpled. A doll's legs stuck up in the air. A book called *My Antonia* lay facedown near Irma Lee's feet.

"Irma Lee?"

She didn't move.

Her jacks were scattered on the wooden floor just beyond the round rug. The little ball lay between the stilts. I picked it up and sat on the floor by the jacks, which I gathered and scattered again. I threw the ball into the air and picked up a jack. The ball bounced twice before I got it.

I felt dumb playing a girl's game. If Irma Lee didn't sit up soon, I was going to stop and try something else. I threw the ball again. This time I picked up a jack and the ball before it bounced, only with two different hands. I threw again, but the ball went wide. I threw again.

"Nuts!" The jack was jammed between two floorboards, and the ball skipped toward the window.

I heard something and looked up. Irma Lee was leaning over the edge of the bed watching me. A tear stood on the tip of her nose, but she was giggling.

I chased after the ball and threw it at her. She caught it and tossed it back. She was fast! So there we were, playing catch, the fastest game of catch I ever played. She was grinning, looking so happy that staring at her made me miss the ball.

She laughed while I went after it. "I made you miss!" And when I came back she said, "More!" And we were off again. Till she let the ball whiz by her and leaned back and laughed and laughed.

After a minute or two, she scrambled to the foot of her bed and opened the toy chest. She pulled out a long flat box. "Want to play checkers?"

I hated checkers. It was a stupid game. "Sure."

"You can be black." She turned the box over and let everything fall to the floor.

I wanted to do something to make her sure we were friends. I was going to be her friend forever, no matter what. She was the only person who wanted me. Not my uncles and aunts, not Ida, not Gideon, not even Solly.

Once, when my friend Ben and I were eight, we each cut our fingers and held the cuts together to make us blood brothers. I wanted to do something like that, but I didn't want Irma Lee to have to cut herself.

She unfolded the checkerboard and started to arrange her pieces.

I spat into my hand. "Spit into my hand," I said.

She looked up, surprised, but did it, no questions asked.

"Give me your hand." I took her right hand and rubbed the palm against my palm. "Now we can't stop being friends, ever."

She rubbed her palms together and then took my other hand and rubbed our spit into it. "Double!"

She was exactly perfect!

I laid out my checkers pieces and moved one forward. "I know how to get into Mr. Doom's office. Tomorrow I'll—"

The door opened and Solly and Mrs. Packer came in. "Baby gi—"

"We just started playing, Mama."

"Boychik, it's past Bandit's bedtime. We should—"

"Tell for you your fortune?" the parrot squawked.

It was four in the morning. The chauffeur was waiting outside. I told him where to drop me off: on 136th Street, by the tree with the rope. Then I sat in the back with Solly and Bandit. The back was almost as good as the front, with the heater under the seat to keep us warm, the thick carpet, and the roses, real live roses, in little vases next to the door hinges.

On the wall near my head was a compartment, and one just like it next to Solly. I opened the one on my side.

"Look!"

A jar of assorted nuts, two glasses, a bottle of liquor, and chocolates wrapped in silver paper. Solly opened the one next to him. Lipstick, powder, perfume, a book of fairy tales, and a clown hand puppet.

The car stopped at the oak tree. The chauffeur opened my door, and Solly got out with me.

"Don't break your neck, boychik."

"Would you stay and see if any lights come on after I go in? If they do, I could use some shmeering."

"I'll take care of it."

I got over the fence and back into the asylum, no problem. The poker game was still going on. I took the nearest staircase, tiptoed upstairs and into our room. Where I lived with my buddies.

I fell asleep imagining showing the carving to Irma Lee and the elevens and Solly, with Bandit squawking, "Mazel! Mazel tov!"

CHAPTER
35

M R. DOOM DIDN'T leave his door unlocked the next day, and the maid didn't clean. But he did the day after, Wednesday. From the top of the marble stairs in the lobby, I watched him leave without locking up.

According to Louis and Danny, the maid came right away after Mr. Doom left, and it took her about ten minutes to clean. Then he came back fifteen minutes or so after she finished. But they were just guessing, because neither of them had a watch.

I started counting seconds as soon as he closed the door. It was easy. I just kept track of my heart pounding. Blam one. Blam two.

Blam three hundred. Five minutes, and the maid still hadn't come. By now I could have opened the cabinet, gotten the carving, and been out of there. Blam six hundred, and she *still* hadn't come.

Blam six hundred and forty-eight, and a maid came out of the stairwell carrying a feather duster and pulling a Hoover. She strolled toward Mr. Doom's office, taking her own sweet time.

She opened the door, went inside, and I started counting again. If she took a whole ten minutes I'd only have five before Mr. Doom came back, and I didn't know if that was enough.

She was out when I got to three hundred and eighty-five, about six minutes. I started down the stairs, still counting. A prefect opened the door from one of the stairwells. I froze. He went into the side hallway. He had stopped me for twenty-five seconds. I had eight minutes left. I could probably do it twice in eight minutes. I continued down the stairs, starting a new count. Blam one. Blam two.

Don't let anybody come into the HHB. Don't let anybody come through the hall.

Nobody did. I opened the door to the office and closed it behind me, fast. Blam eighteen. I smelled furniture polish.

Blam twenty-one. My hand was shaking so bad I couldn't get the key into the lock and then I dropped it. Blam twenty-five. Don't rush. You're making it worse. Take a deep breath. Try again. Blam twenty-nine.

I heard footsteps. I dove for the kneehole of the desk. The footsteps got louder, passed the door, and got softer.

I'd lost count of the seconds. The key went in. I tried to turn it. It wouldn't turn. Was it the wrong key? I jiggled it. The lock moved. It was the right key! I pulled. The door stuck for a second, then opened. The glass rattled.

More footsteps.

I took out the carving. I touched Papa.

I moved a china donkey, a bowl of seashells, and a wooden box to fill in the empty space on the shelf. Now I'd just put the key back in the desk—

The door opened. Mr. Doom!

"Whaa? Whoo?" he roared. He blocked the door. Black shape in the doorway. Light around him.

He wasn't getting the carving back! I hugged it to my chest. *He wasn't going to beat me again!* I rushed at him. Jumped—leaped. Reached up. Threw his specs over my shoulder. Threw the key.

Had to get out. He was yelling—words, sounds. "Where . . . You won't . . . Can't see . . . Just let me . . ."

I dodged him. His arms were going up, down, sideways—hunting. I sprang back. He wouldn't get out of the way.

Between his legs. I was a bullet. A cannonball. I hurtled through. He shouted, grabbed. He had my foot. I pulled. Kept going. I was through. He had my shoe.

People running. Mr. Meltzer. Other prefects. Boys. I shot across the lobby. A boy opened the front door for me—older—not an eleven. He had green eyes. Funny how I noticed.

I was out—outside. It was raining. Sleeting. I ran through the gate, and kept going. My shoeless foot— cold, *cold!* Ran toward Broadway. Stepped on something sharp—ouch! Kept running. Three prefects—Mr. Meltzer—behind me. Half a block. Mr. Meltzer catching up. Out of breath. A quarter block—

Broadway—people—peddler's cart—laundry wagon— taxi—trolley at a stop. Trolley! People getting on. Mr. Meltzer at the corner. I ran into the street. One more to get on. I stood behind the trolley. *Hurry up, mister. Get on!* He did. *Start! Start!* The trolley moved. I jumped onto the back bumper. Almost dropped the carving.

Good-bye, Mr. Meltzer.

I hung on to the back of the trolley window with my right hand and clutched the carving with the other. My teeth were chattering.

I didn't have a cent. My money was back at the HHB. The trolley was heading downtown.

Where could I go? Nowhere.

It was a laugh. When I wanted to run away, I had to stay. And when I wanted to stay, I had to go.

I looked down at the carving, at Papa and Mama and Gideon and me, waiting on line to get on the ark. The family we should have been. The trolley lurched, and I held on with both hands, the carving between my elbows and my chest. Then the trolley steadied, and I looked at the bottom of my shoeless foot to see if I'd cut it. Miraculously, no blood was seeping through the sock.

The trolley stopped. The conductor was getting out to chase me. I jumped off into a freezing puddle and ran.

I was safe from Mr. Doom, and I had the carving, but I'd never see my buddies again.

It took me over four hours to reach my old neighborhood. After the first trolley, I jumped on anything I could, mostly trolleys, and stayed on till the driver chased me off. If a furniture truck driver hadn't let me ride inside with him from 60th Street to Houston Street, I might have frozen to death.

I had decided to go to Aunt Sarah and Aunt Lily's. As soon as the truck driver dropped me off, I knew I was home. I could have been blind and I would have known. It was the stink. Garbage and crap—horse crap and people crap. In all the times I'd thought about home, I hadn't thought once about the smell.

It was a quarter to six when I got to Aunt Lily and Aunt Sarah's building on Eldridge Street. I wished they weren't boarders. It was going to be bad enough telling them what had happened without the whole Cohen family hearing it too. The hallway seemed narrower and darker than I remembered. I climbed the stairs, hugging the carving and trying to make my teeth stop chattering.

I had loused everything up. I should have waited for a day when the maid came right away. I should have just watched to see what happened, to see if it went the way Louis and Danny had said. I could have waited. There was no emergency.

I knocked on the door.

"Who could that be?" Mrs. Cohen opened the door. "Dave? Is that you? Dave Caros? You're soaking wet. Come in."

I went in and stood, dripping on the cracked linoleum in their kitchen. It was warm in here. I sneezed. Mrs. Cohen had been washing one of her boys in the washtub next to the sink. There were soapsuds in his hair, and he started crying.

Aunt Sarah rushed to me from the front room. "Dave! What happened?"

Aunt Lily was right behind her. "You're drenched."

Mr. Cohen and another son came out of the bedroom. The two little girls stood in the doorway to the front room. They all stared at me.

Aunt Sarah hurried back into the front room. "I'll get a towel."

Mrs. Cohen started rinsing the crying kid in the tub. "It's all right," she crooned.

The Cohens' apartment seemed tiny, but it was the same size as our old place. I didn't remember our apartment being so small.

"Where's your shoe? Sarah, he's missing a shoe."

Aunt Sarah came back. I handed Papa's carving to her. "Aah, pyew, he's filthy. Get me a washcloth, Lily. Take your clothes off, Dave."

"I'll just be a minute." Mrs. Cohen got her kid out

of the tub, and I started washing myself at the sink. At the Home we had hot water.

Mrs. Cohen shooed her daughters into the front room. "We'll give you some privacy." Mr. Cohen and his sons went back into the bedroom. I was alone in the kitchen with Aunt Sarah and Aunt Lily, but it wasn't private. Everybody could hear everything.

After I finished at the sink, Aunt Sarah washed my shirt. Aunt Lily brushed as much of the mud as she could off my jacket and knickers. Then she put something on the stove to heat. Aunt Sarah gave me two towels to wrap myself in and told me to sit at the table. In a few minutes Aunt Lily handed me a bowl of hot spinach-and-bean soup. Aunt Sarah draped my clothes over the stove to dry.

"Where's Papa's carving?" I asked.

"I washed it too," Aunt Lily said, pointing. It was on the floor near the door, drying on newspapers.

"Dave," Aunt Sarah said, "what did you do this time?"

I told them. They thought I shouldn't have gone into Mr. Doom's office. And they thought I should have stayed and apologized when I was caught. Neither of them believed me about the beating I would have gotten. They didn't even think Mr. Doom had been stealing when he took Papa's carving.

"He was just keeping it safe for you," Aunt Lily said.

"It's not as if you're a paying customer," Aunt Sarah added.

When I finished my soup and some bread, Aunt Lily asked Aunt Sarah, "Can't he stay here tonight? I hate to go out again."

From the front room Mrs. Cohen called out, "Certainly he can stay tonight. No charge."

But Aunt Sarah took my clothes off the stove. "They probably called the police. We have to take him right away."

I should have known better than to come here. I should have known they'd bring me back.

CHAPTER
36

"WHAT ARE WE going to put on his feet?"
Aunt Lily asked. "He can't go barefoot."
She started giggling.

Aunt Sarah laughed too. "He looked like a drowned rat when he came in."

I wasn't going back.

My clothes were still damp, but they were warm. The sock I'd walked on all day was more hole than sock. They gave me Aunt Lily's galoshes to wear instead of shoes. She said it didn't matter if her feet got wet.

The galoshes were too big, but Aunt Sarah tied them around my ankles with string. Mrs. Cohen lent me her oilcloth tablecloth for a raincoat. I wrapped it around myself and held the carving safe underneath.

At the bottom of the stairs, Aunt Lily took my hand. As soon as we got outside, I yanked free and ran.

Aunt Sarah hollered, "Dave! Get back here! Catch that boy! Get him!"

Aunt Lily yelled, "Dave, don't go!" And then, "Be careful."

The aunts were too slow to catch me and nobody else tried. The streets were less crowded than usual because of the weather, but they were still crowded. It had gotten colder, and it was starting to snow.

When I was sure they weren't behind me, I took the oilcloth off. If Aunt Lily and Aunt Sarah reported me, the police wouldn't have any trouble finding a boy wearing a plaid tablecloth. Instead, I wrapped the oilcloth around the carving and carried it under my arm.

Where could I go? Uncle Milt and Aunt Fanny lived only two blocks away, but Aunt Fanny was always sick.

I circled around to our old building on Ludlow Street. It was about nine o'clock. Ike, the produce peddler, was still hawking his fruit. The peddler Ida used to buy soap from was there too. A light was on in our front room. I wondered who lived there now.

Papa, I thought, *what should I do?*

I remembered what Gideon had said right before he left, that I'd be all right. That I was always all right. Well, I wasn't all right now.

The appetizing store was open and so was the candy store. Mr. Schwartz and Mr. Goldfarb knew me, and Mr. Schwartz was nice. He might give me a pickle. But he wouldn't invite me to live with him.

I started walking again, not knowing where I was going.

A woman stuck her head out of a window and hollered for her son, David. My name, not my mama. Her David hollered back, "Five more minutes. Please, Mama."

Papa, what should I do? Nobody wants me.

I sneezed. If I was dry, if I wasn't so cold, if I had somewhere to stay tonight, I could plan. I could think of something.

Then I remembered that Solly lived on Stanton Street. He didn't want me either, but I was sure he wouldn't take me back to Mr. Doom tonight. I turned around and started toward Stanton Street.

Stanton was long. I didn't know the number, and Solly might not be home. I'd never find him.

And then I had an idea.

I stood in the middle of the street—no cars were coming—and I waited for a quiet second—a somewhat quiet second. Then I hollered as loud as I could, "Tell for you your fortune?"

Nothing happened. Peddlers went on yelling. People went on bargaining, calling to each other. No Solly. And no one asked me for a fortune.

Farther down the block I tried again, and nothing happened again. I kept going. On each block I yelled once at each end. And on each block everyone ignored me. On Allen Street I waited for the train to rumble by before

I hollered. Nothing. I might as well not have waited.

I kept going.

"Tell for you your fortune?" Stanton Street ran out in three more blocks.

"Tell for you your fortune?" Stanton Street ran out in two more blocks.

Stanton Street ran out. I turned back to try again. I couldn't think of anything else to do. Or anywhere else to go.

I was heading toward Pitt Street when I thought I heard "Boychik!" I whirled around. I didn't see Solly anywhere. A peddler called out, "Hot chestnuts!" I must have imagined it. I started walking again. But then I heard a parrot squawk, "Tell for you your fortune?" I turned and started back.

Then I saw Solly's head sticking out a second-story window. "Boychik! Is that you?"

"Yes!"

"Come on up. No. Better, I'll come down and get you." His head vanished.

I waited on the sidewalk, shivering.

"Come in. Come in." Solly, in a yellow bathrobe, held the building door open.

I followed him upstairs.

"Mazel tov. Welcome home!" Bandit squawked.

"You're a block of ice. Sit down." Solly pointed to a kitchen chair. "I'll be right back." He went into the front room and came back with a blanket. "Get undressed and wrap yourself in this."

I put the oilcloth with the carving down on the table and took off my wet clothes. Then I wrapped myself in the blanket and looked around. From here I could see into the front room. Along one wall were stacks of brown cardboard boxes. Then, in front of the boxes were stacks of newspapers. Pushed against the wall across from the kitchen was a piano. Books were piled on the floor under the keyboard and on top of the bench. I didn't see how anybody could play it. On top of the piano were framed photographs and Solly's hat.

Solly was at the stove, looking for matches. I picked up the oilcloth with the carving inside and went into the front room to see the photographs. With the blanket wrapped around me, I felt like an Indian chief. A cold, shivering one.

The biggest picture was of a woman with frizzy hair, a long nose, and a lopsided smile. I liked the smile. She wasn't just smiling at the camera, she was smiling because something was funny. A minute ago she had been laughing her head off and she was still smiling when the photographer took the picture. Next to it was a picture of a boy on a pony.

Papa once had our pictures taken like that. I'd kicked my pony, hoping he'd gallop.

"How about some chicken soup?"

"Okay." I went back to the kitchen.

Solly put a light under a pot and then sat down at the table. "So why are you telling fortunes on Stanton Street?"

I didn't want to talk about how I'd messed everything up. "I changed my mind about staying at the HHB. I ran away for good."

"Just like that?"

"Just like that."

"You ran away with a tablecloth?" He pointed to it in my lap.

"It's not a tablecloth. I mean, it is, but it has something in it." I didn't show him.

He went to the stove to ladle out my soup. "Let it cool a minute." He sat down across from me. "Nu? So what are your plans?"

I shrugged. "Can I stay here tonight?"

"Certainly. I'll set you up in front of the stove. You'll sleep like a baby."

At least he was better than Aunt Sarah and Aunt Lily.

"More soup?"

"Okay. Thanks."

He brought it to me and sat down again. He was silent for a minute, and then he snapped his fingers.

Bandit squawked, "Oy vay! Gevalt!"

Solly said, "That paskudnyak did something, no?"

I shrugged again, looking down at his linoleum. I looked up. He was watching me, concentrating on me. His expression was more serious than usual, almost completely serious. He was worried about me.

I decided to tell him what had happened. It couldn't hurt. I had nothing to lose. I unfolded the oilcloth so Solly could see the carving.

He reached for it, then stopped. "May I?" I nodded, and he picked it up. He studied it and ran his fingers over the wood. "This is a work of art, Daveleh."

Now why did that make me cry? He says the carving is a work of art, which I knew already, and I start crying my head off. "My papa made it," I managed to get out. And then I felt worse. For some reason I felt like Papa died yesterday instead of almost two months ago.

"Oy vay! Oy gevalt!" Bandit squawked.

I finally caught my breath. "Mr. Doom—the paskudnyak—stole it from me." And I told him the whole story—about my things in the suitcase, about the beating and taking Mr. Doom's glasses, about getting the key to the cabinet, about the twins being beaten up too. I even told him about Mr. Doom's speech before he beat me up and before he beat the twins up.

He said "Oy vay" once or twice, but mostly he listened. When I told what happened today, it didn't sound like I loused up so much. It sounded more like I got unlucky with the maid being late and Mr. Doom being early.

"So that's why I tried to find you," I finished. "To stay somewhere tonight."

"I knew that stinker was a paskudnyak. Your soup is cold. I'll get you more hot." He went to the stove. "You want to live there because of your buddies?" He went into the next room, probably his bedroom.

"Uh-huh. And the art teacher is going to give me special lessons."

He came back with a jacket and pants and got dressed. "The alrightniks could fix the superintendent," he said, "but they'd meddle and make something else worse, and I don't want to give them the satisfaction. I have a better idea since you told me the paskudnyak is interested in high society." He got his hat from the piano and started for the door. "I'll be back soon. No, wait." He took a plate and silverware off the shelf over the stove. "When you finish the soup there's chicken in the pot. Help yourself. Bandit will keep you company." He left.

CHAPTER
37

I FINISHED THE SOUP. There wasn't much flavor left in the chicken, and it was like eating a towel, but I ate it anyway. My eyes stung from crying so much. Maybe Solly's idea, whatever it was, would help me. I was too tired to wonder about it.

After I ate, I wandered back to the piano. I leaned over the books to press a few keys. It sounded jangly, and I wished I knew how to play. I picked up one of the books on the bench, *The Prophet,* by somebody named Kahlil Gibran. I read a sentence about love and secrets of the heart. Not interesting. I picked up another book. *I and Thou* by Martin Buber. I put it down too and yawned.

I fell asleep on the couch and didn't hear Solly come back. In fact, I didn't hear anything till morning when Bandit's squawking woke me.

Sun streamed in the front room window. I was warm and dry on the couch cushion in front of the stove. Solly must have moved me.

He was at the table, drinking coffee and reading a newspaper. He didn't know I was awake, so I could watch him. He nodded at something in the paper, and his cheeks jiggled.

He had been kinder to me than anybody else, even though he wouldn't let me stay with him. He'd given me a lot of reasons for not letting me stay, but he'd never said he didn't want me. I hadn't believed his reasons, because everyone I knew had reasons for not taking me. And everybody's reasons boiled down to not wanting me. But maybe Solly was different.

"Solly?" I said. My voice sounded husky. "If you thought you could keep me, would you want to?"

"You're awake, Daveleh? Good morning." He sipped his coffee. "I thought you wanted to stay at your HHB."

That wasn't an answer. Yes, it was. He didn't want me.

He shook his head. "No, I should answer. You asked a good question. If I could adopt you, boychik, and I had a signed letter from a higher authority that I would stay healthy, I would want to. I would like to find out if everybody I raise turns into an alrightnik."

"Oh." I leaned back on the couch cushion. I felt like crying again. I wanted to thank him, but I didn't know what to say. So instead I asked, "What's an alrightnik?"

He put down his cup. "An alrightnik is somebody who forgets that he wasn't born a doctor or a judge or a businessman. He forgets that a lot of people made it possible for him to get so high-and-mighty."

I understood. Mr. Doom was an alrightnik. It was better to be a gonif like Solly.

I stood up and went out to the toilet in the hall and waited behind two other people to get in.

When I came back, Solly said, "Boychik, you want a slice of rye bread? An apple? A cup of tea?"

I nodded. "What time is it?" It could be afternoon. It could be next week.

"A quarter to nine."

Mr. Cluck would have started his morning lecture. Mike would already have drawn a few violins. This afternoon I would have been in Mr. Hillinger's special art class.

Solly stood at the stove, making my breakfast. "Odelia Packer will be here at nine-thirty."

"She will?"

He carried a plate to the table. "Eat. I'll pour your tea. Should I put honey in it?"

"Why is she coming?"

"We're taking you to your HHB in style. Honey?"

I nodded about the honey. Yesterday I would have thought Solly was taking me back to get rid of me, like Aunt Sarah and Aunt Lily had tried to. Now I just wondered what he had up his sleeve.

My clothes were draped over the oven. I got into

them. They were dry and warm and even stiffer than usual.

"We're going to settle that paskudnyak."

I grinned. "How?"

"You'll see. I'm looking forward to it."

"Is Irma Lee coming?"

"Her mama didn't say."

I looked down at myself. It was hard to wrinkle an HHB jacket, since it was mostly made of iron, but I had managed. It was full of wrinkles, except for the spots that were covered with caked mud. My knickers were just as bad, plus they had a rip in the side. "You don't have any boy's clothes, do you?"

"No, Daveleh. Eat your breakfast."

Irma Lee had said I looked swell in pajamas. Maybe she'd think I looked swell in mud.

At twenty-five after nine Solly, Bandit, and I went downstairs to wait for Mrs. Packer. To keep me warm, Solly had lent me his other suit jacket, the one he wasn't wearing. It covered my muddy jacket and knickers, but it had a brown stain on the lapel, and it was much too big.

I had the carving under my arm, but I'd left the oilcloth on Solly's kitchen table. He'd promised to return it to Mrs. Cohen and to tell Aunt Lily and Aunt Sarah that I'd gone back to the HHB. I said he should tell my aunts that I found a million-dollar bill on Delancey Street and had moved into the Waldorf.

It was warm for December, and it was sunny. The snow had turned to slush, but my feet were dry in Aunt Lily's galoshes.

While we waited I started thinking. Except for Papa, nobody had ever been as kind to me as Solly. He'd even missed his gonifing last night because of me. I thought about who was nice—Solly, the nurse, Irma Lee—and who wasn't, which was a longer list. My relatives, for example. Gideon, for example. He had no good reason for leaving me behind, for leaving me to be given away like a used undershirt.

I imagined him at the HHB. He'd have been bully chopped meat. I grinned, but then I stopped grinning in surprise. I was being an alrightnik about Gideon! Well, not exactly, but close. To get along at the HHB, you had to be tough, a rascal. You had to be like me, which Gideon wasn't.

Moe and the other bullies were Gideon's age. He wouldn't be able to handle them, no matter how much of a genius he was. If he lived at the Home, they'd cream him over and over again.

Solly said, "Are you warm enough, boychik?"

"Uh-huh."

It would be worse for me too with Gideon there. I would try to help him, and I would feel terrible that he had given up his chance to live with Uncle Jack. Even though I would have stayed with him if Uncle Jack or another relative had picked me instead. We were different, so it wouldn't be right for us to act the same identical way.

Gideon hadn't just left me here either. He'd gone on writing to me every week, even though I'd never written back. He'd given me Papa's carving, which had always been his most treasured—

"There it is," Solly said.

I owe Gideon a letter, I thought. I could send him some drawings too.

Solly's watch said it was five to ten. As soon as I saw the Cadillac I got scared. Maybe they wouldn't settle Mr. Doom and he would settle us.

I thought people would stare when the chauffeur opened the door for us, but they didn't. Well, one person did—a girl, about three years old, who was standing near the curb with both fists stuffed in her mouth. Everyone else acted like they rode in chauffeured limousines three times a week.

We got in, and there was Irma Lee, sitting on one of the jump seats and smiling at me. She was wearing a blue coat, white gloves, and a round little blue hat. I couldn't imagine how she could look prettier.

"Get in, boychik."

I took the other jump seat, and held the carving on my lap. Solly sank into the upholstery next to Mrs. Packer.

"Mama says we're going to scare the pants off your bad old superintendent," Irma Lee said before the chauffeur even closed the door behind us.

Mrs. Packer laughed. "Baby girl, we are going to scare him and hope his pants stay right where they should be."

On the way uptown, Irma Lee held Papa's carving on her lap and examined it, saying "ooh" and "ah" every so often, and laughing at the monkey on the leopard's back. When she was done, she said, "Mama, look," and gave it to Mrs. Packer. Solly told them my papa had done the carving, and Mrs. Packer said it was no wonder I was interested in art.

Irma Lee started telling me something. I think it was about a cousin of hers who was an aviator. I couldn't pay attention. I kept worrying. How were an old man, a bird, a lady, and a little girl going to scare Mr. Doom?

We turned onto 136th Street. There was an inch of snow on the ground up here. A rope hung from my tree, and I wondered how it had gotten there. Then I knew. My buddies had snuck out last night and put it there in case I came back. They were the best.

We turned onto Amsterdam Avenue and drew up in front of the Humble House of Buddies. The chauffeur opened the car door.

We walked up the brick path to the door. The path was slick from melting snow. I almost slipped and dropped the carving.

Solly held the door open for us. This was it.

CHAPTER 38

THE LOBBY WAS empty.

"Where do we go, boychik?"

I pointed to Mr. Doom's office. The door was shut as usual. We walked toward it. Mrs. Packer's heels clacked on the tiles and echoed off the walls.

Solly knocked, and Mr. Doom rumbled that we should come in. I got ready to run. Solly put his arm around my shoulder.

There he was—Mr. Doom—huge as ever, mean as ever. He looked up and saw me. His left hand went up to hold his glasses in place. He smiled a fake smile. "Dave! We've been so worried." He stood. "Thank you for bringing Dave home," he told Solly. "Excuse me for a moment." He went to the phone on the wall and told the operator to call the police station.

He was going to have me arrested! I tried to get

away, but Solly held me tight.

Mr. Doom said into the telephone, "Please tell Officer Kelly that our boy came home. He's with me right now, safe and sound." He hung up and came around the desk to shake Solly's hand.

"Mazel. Mazel tov," the parrot squawked.

Mr. Doom backed up a step. "Beautiful bird. I love birds. You are Dave's . . . ?" He paused, waiting for Solly to answer.

"His grandpa."

"And these . . ."—he nodded at Mrs. Packer and Irma Lee—". . . are your maids?"

How could Mrs. Packer scare him if he thought she was a maid?

Irma Lee started giggling. Mrs. Packer looked like she was trying not to laugh. I didn't see what was so funny.

Mr. Doom continued. "I'm surprised you left Dave with us if—"

"I'm not a rich man," Solly said.

Mr. Doom frowned, trying to figure it out. Then he gave up the riddle. "Dave, why did you run away?"

I didn't answer.

"Take off your coat, son." He reached for Papa's carving. "I'll hold this."

I hugged the carving tight against my chest. He wasn't getting it.

"Gozlin! Holdupnik!" Bandit squawked.

Mr. Doom shrugged. "I just don't want you to get overheated. Mr. Caros—"

"Gruber. Solomon Gruber. And my boss here is Mrs. Odelia Packer."

"Odelia Packer! *The* Odelia Pa—" Mr. Doom rushed at her. "Madam, I'm so sorry. I didn't recognize you." He straightened his suit jacket. "I'm honored to have you as a guest. Wait till I tell Mrs. Bloom! She reads to me about your salons. Did Baron Rothschild . . ." He held out his hand, which Mrs. Packer didn't take.

"Mr. Gruber has told me shocking things about the institution you run here," Mrs. Packer said.

"Mada—"

"If something happened to me, and my baby—my daughter had to live in a place—"

"God forbid something should—"

"I would be spinning in my grave. Spinning! Inedible food! The poor boys are freezing to death. And their precious . . ."—she reached for Papa's carving; I let her have it—". . . keepsakes are taken from them."

"Mada—"

"Mr. Gruber would care for his grandson himself, but his health is too uncertain . . ."

Was this part true? I thought of how out of breath he got from climbing stairs, and how slowly he always walked. I looked at him, but I couldn't tell. He was too busy being a gonif, nodding seriously at everything Mrs. Packer said.

"Madam, I deeply re—"

"Mr. Gruber handles my charitable work." She turned to Solly. "I believe a board of directors oversees . . ."

Solly said, "I saw Norman Rosen yesterday, just a few hours before Daveleh came, dripping—"

"Sir! I never intended . . . If I had only known . . ." Beads of sweat were gathering on Mr. Doom's forehead.

"Mr. Gruber can speak to Mr. Rosen tomorrow and tell him what happened—"

"No, madam! He can't—I mean, he mustn't. The boy will be treated . . . Dave . . ." He smiled at me. He was begging. "I meant no harm. I thought—"

"You stole my papa's carving and called him a bum." It felt grand to tell him off. "You're the bum, you're the thief, you're the paskud—"

"Enough, boychik. Mr. Bloom gets the idea."

Mr. Doom crouched in front of me. "Dave, will you accept my sincere, my sincerest apologies?"

"Oy vay," the parrot squawked. "Gevalt!"

There was nothing sincere about him. "Just stay away from my things, and leave us elevens alone."

Mrs. Packer waved her hand. "Mr. Gruber and I know how difficult it is to run a large institution. Never enough money, never enough help . . ."

Mr. Doom nodded as she spoke. "Never enough money," he echoed. He stood up. "Madam, if you would interest yourself in our mission, to bring up these chil—"

"Mr. Gruber?"

"Since Dave was here, I didn't feel right about suggesting a donation, but I think they could use a new furnace."

For a second Mrs. Packer looked blank. Then she chuckled. "A new furnace."

Solly was gonifing her too, to get us a furnace!

She was trying not to laugh. "We'll look into it. Perhaps we can discuss it further when we come back to visit."

"Delighted, madam. Delighted. Any time."

"When are visiting days, Dave?"

I told her, and she promised to come.

We left Mr. Doom's office then, and they all—including Mr. Doom—walked with me to Mr. Cluck's classroom. I didn't like walking anywhere near him. I had told him off, and it felt good, but I wished Solly and Mrs. Packer could stay a little longer, like a few years longer. I wished Mr. Doom had signed an oath swearing he wouldn't touch me again.

When we reached the classroom, we stood outside and shook hands with Mr. Doom. I expected him to squeeze my hand extra hard to show me what to expect later, but he didn't. It was like shaking hands with a dead fish.

When I shook Mrs. Packer's hand, she said, "When we come next Sunday, Dave, I'll expect a full report. If anything is wrong, your grandfather and I want to hear about it."

"Nothing will be wrong, madam. I guarantee it."

I promised to tell her and thanked her for bringing me back. Then I turned to Solly. "Is your health really poor, Grandpa?"

"I'm not getting any younger, boychik," he said, "but I'm sound as a bell. Don't I look like a bell?"

I grinned and shook my head.

"Don't worry. I'll live to dance at your first art show. And you can show me your drawings on Visiting Day."

I shook Irma Lee's hand too. "Good-bye. See you." I couldn't think of anything else, even though I hadn't said nearly enough.

She whispered in my ear, "We're having another party in two weeks. You'll come if you're my friend, Dave Caros."

I grinned. Then they left, and I went inside to join my buddies.

After they'd gone, I was jumpy all day. I knew Mr. Doom would want to beat me more than ever. He'd be sure to hate me for scaring him with Solly and Mrs. Packer.

But he didn't touch me. Not that day or the next, or the one after that. On Sunday, Visiting Day, Solly and Irma Lee and her mama came. Mr. Doom pounced on Mrs. Packer in the lobby, and she had to listen to him for almost a half hour. But then we went upstairs so Irma Lee could meet the elevens. At first everybody was shy, including me. But then I thought of going out in the courtyard for a game of tag. Irma Lee was in heaven, and she was as fast as the best of us. And I was proud to show her off to my buddies.

Mrs. Packer didn't buy us a new furnace, but at the beginning of January she sent the HHB forty quilts exclusively for the elevens.

After a while, when I was convinced that Mr. Doom wouldn't touch me, I began to practice my gonifing on him. I'd go right up to him and say, "Mrs. Packer asked me to tell you hello." And then, if I was with another eleven, I'd introduce him. I'd say, "This is Mike," or "This is Eli," and I'd add, "He's my special buddy, so I hope you'll take good care of him, Mr. Bloom, sir."

And Mr. Doom would shake my buddy's hand and my hand and tell me to send his regards to Mrs. Packer.

So we were safe, all of us elevens. Nobody else was, though, until the nice nurse got fed up and went to the HHB board of directors about a month after I ran away. They investigated and fired Mr. Doom. We got a new superintendent, Mr. Dresher. The food wasn't any tastier, and we were still cold, but at least he didn't beat anybody.

About three months after Mr. Doom left, Eli got a letter from Alfie. He had learned how to milk a cow. "The first time I tried it," he wrote, "the cow stepped on my toe, and I saw stars. But now I'm good at it. They make me drink so much milk here I can't look a glass of milk in the eye anymore." He said he had gained five pounds, and the doctor said he was holding his own, even though he was still coughing.

We didn't know what to think about that. Some of us thought it sounded bad. Some thought it sounded good. Harvey said it was Alfie's death sentence for sure. But anyway, Eli wrote back to him. We all added a few lines, and I put in a drawing of Mr. Cluck to make him laugh.

I took the special art lessons from Mr. Hillinger, and I liked them very much. Very very much. I did more gesture drawings and used watercolors and oil paints and even tried sculpture. About six months after the first special lesson, I did a drawing of Irma Lee that I wasn't too ashamed of. Mrs. Packer called it "Baby Girl's Portrait," and she put it in a golden frame and hung it in their dining room.

Mrs. Packer and Irma Lee didn't come every Sunday, but Solly never missed a Visiting Day. Plus I met him often in the middle of the night at the Tree of Hope. He said I was the best groaner in Harlem.

Tell for you your fortune?

AFTERWORD

My father grew up in the Hebrew Orphan Asylum, which was known as the HOA to the kids who lived there. It was a real orphanage located in the same place as the HHB, which I invented.

My father's name when he was born was David Carasso, although he changed Carasso to Carson when he was old enough, so he would be a "real American." His mother died from childbirth complications when he was a few months old. His father, Abraham Carasso, died of gangrene after a cut he'd gotten in his carpentry work became infected. Abraham truly did build a cabinet with secret compartments for the sultan of Turkey, and he truly did receive a medal, or so family lore has it. After Abraham died, my father, his older brother, Sam, and his younger half-brother, Leo, were placed in the HOA. My father's sisters and his older brother, Sidney, went to live with relatives.

My father was much younger than eleven when he arrived at the HOA, although I don't know exactly how young he was. Some children liked the HOA, but my father hated it. Many years later, he would tell my sister and me almost nothing about it, even though we were dying to know about the exciting childhood of our safe, respectable daddy. One of the few tales he did tell was of sneaking out of the orphanage to buy candy. He had a thriving candy business in the HOA, till he got caught and had to declare bankruptcy!

After he left the Home, my father had nothing more to do with the place, until he and my mother retired. One day, a man recognized him on the street and turned out to be one of his HOA pals. After that, my father joined the HOA alumni association and was a member until he died in 1986.

There are many differences between the fictional HHB and the real HOA. An important one is that the HOA took in both boys and girls. Another big difference is that relatives couldn't bring children directly to the HOA; the children had to be placed there through a legal process. As far as I know, the superintendents at the HOA were not monsters like Mr. Doom, but discipline was strict, and punishments were severe. There is a wonderful book about the HOA called *The Luckiest Orphans* by Hyman Bogen, published by the University of Illinois Press. The HOA closed its doors in 1941. Its most famous alumnus is the newspaper columnist Art Buchwald.

Although all the characters in *Dave at Night* are completely fictional, parties or salons were held during the Harlem Renaissance of the 1920s and '30s that were attended by leading figures in the arts, both black and white. A'lelia Walker, who inherited the hair-straightening-products fortune of her mother, Madame C. J. Walker, was a prominent hostess of the day. The crown prince of Sweden did try to attend one of her parties and was unable to get in. *Noah's Ark*, the painting by Aaron Douglas that Dave admires during Irma

Lee's party, was actually painted in 1927.

Two excellent books about Harlem are *When Harlem Was in Vogue* by David Levering Lewis, published by Knopf, and *This Was Harlem* by Jervis Anderson, published by Farrar, Straus & Giroux. *You Must Remember This* by Jeff Kisseloff, published by Schocken Books, is a delightful history of Manhattan from the 1890s to World War II.

Like Dave, I know only a few Yiddish words and phrases, so Solly's Yiddish came from *The Joys of Yiddish* by Leo Rosten, which is published by Pocket Books, and which has many jokes along with the definitions.